One Good Man

Marie McGaha

ONE GOOD MAN

Marie McGaha

Marie McGaha

Publishers Note:

This is a work of fiction. All names, characters, places, and events are the work of the author's imagination. Any resemblance to real persons, places, or events is coincidental.

Cover Art: Val Muller

Copyright ©Marie McGaha 2012
All rights reserved
ISBN 13: 978-0615723174
ISBN 10: 0615723179

ONE GOOD MAN

Marie McGaha

ONE GOOD MAN

Marie McGaha

ONE GOOD MAN

Marie McGaha

Marie McGaha

For all the good men in my life

ONE GOOD MAN

Marie McGaha

Marie McGaha

~ One ~

Men were all alike. Selfish. Self-centered. Condescending. Arrogant. And they were cheaters, to boot! Allison Hamstead thought as she stormed around the room, wishing she had something to break. But everything in the room that would break, she'd bought herself, and she wasn't about to destroy her own things. If Wesley Smothers had left any of his stuff there, she'd certainly be breaking it now, although it would be much more satisfying to break Wesley Smothers' leg, arm or, preferably, his neck.

Six months wasted on that cheating pig. Six months of paying the rent and the electric bill. Six months of cooking for him, doing his laundry, and being his fool while he slept with her best friend. And just like that, he'd come home from work one day and told her he didn't think this arrangement was working for him.

Arrangement.

He'd called *her* an arrangement! Oh, she'd like to show him an arrangement or two. And to think, she'd actually been considering marrying him. That was it, the final straw. She hoped a bus would hit him. No, she hoped a bus would hit him and Sarah, both. How could she have been so stupid? So naïve? Such a trusting fool?

Marie McGaha

She had worked with Sarah for two years, and they'd been good friends. Losing Sarah's friendship was worse than losing Wesley, since she hadn't really loved him. Wesley paid so much attention to her, that she had acted like a foolish schoolgirl. Sending him notes with hearts dotting the "i's" and writing *Mrs. Allison Smothers* on her notepad while at work—how lame could she be? Not many men looked at her twice, and especially not men who looked like Wesley. They looked at women like Sarah.

Obviously! How could she have been such an idiot? How was it possible that a relatively intelligent woman could believe such a pig like Wesley?

Allison knew her face was round, but she wasn't ugly. Maybe a little soft around the middle, but at least she wasn't slinky thin like Sarah. Besides, she was on a diet—again, for the millionth time in her life, of course, but still, size sixteen wasn't *that* big for her someone of her height. She *was* five-feet-eight-inches tall after all, and hadn't worn a size six since she *was* six. How many women *actually* wore a size six? From the women she knew, not many. Sure, some were model-thin, but there were a lot of women her age that were much larger than a size six. And hadn't rounded, curvy women been sought after at one time or another in history? How she wished she had lived then—she would've been a superstar.

Sighing, she kicked off her shoes and rubbed her aching toes. Allison had always had a weight

Marie McGaha

problem. She'd weighed over ten pounds when she was born. Fate had been against her from the begining, and she never really had a chance to be thin. Growing up with a mother who was a size four hadn't helped. Her mother hadn't meant to be unkind when Allison was younger, but the fact that her mother was so slim didn't help. Allison knew her mother just didn't understand what it was like to have a weight problem. She restricted her daughter's meals, tried to bribe her with clothing, with money, with everything she could think of, and Allison had just continued to get bigger and bigger. Not even the hypnotist, psychologist, or fat farm helped.

Allison knew she was a disappointment to her mother, but the more Mom worried over Allison's weight, the more Allison seemed to eat. High school had been sheer torture and Allison begged to be home-schooled, but her mother worked two jobs and couldn't take on Allison's education personally. Allison got even bigger over the four years she suffered through high school. The popular girls in gym class laughed at her, and she was constantly late for science class because she hid out until all the other girls had showered and dressed, so she didn't have to undress in front of them.

Allison didn't have a date for the prom, and she didn't get invited to any of the parties the other kids enjoyed. High school was a very lonely time, and her only friend had been a girl with buckteeth and glasses with the opposite problem Allison had.

Marie McGaha

Gloria was so thin, her knees were knobby, and her legs and arms seemed too long for the rest of her body. So on prom night, Allison and Gloria laid on Gloria's bed eating ice cream, cookies, candy, and an assortment of other junk food, while trying to pretend they didn't care. But all the junk food in the world couldn't fill the emptiness Allison felt deep inside.

College hadn't been much better for Allison, especially since Gloria went to a different school. Allison was truly alone then. She had learned to hide her loneliness behind a cheerful smile, and spent her college years tutoring some of those same girls who had gotten through high school on their good looks. It was little comfort, but a small part of Allison delighted in the irony.

After graduation, Allison landed a job with Markham Brothers and later transferred to the company office in Chicago. She thought a new city might make a difference, but it hadn't. Most of the women in the Chicago office looked at Allison with something close to pity in their eyes, and she overheard their comments when they thought she was out of earshot. It wasn't anything she hadn't heard before: *"'She has such a pretty face.' 'If she'd just lose a little weight.' 'How does anyone let themselves get that fat?' 'Where does she find jeans that size?' 'Hasn't she ever heard of Jenny Craig?'"*

Oh yeah, she'd heard every mean thing ever said about her, but she never said anything back to

Marie McGaha

anyone. She just ate more, knowing it wouldn't make her feel better in the end, as it only added to her problem. No matter what the shrinks and the diet counselors said, she didn't care anymore.

Having been on every diet known to man, and a few she came up with on her own, Allison starved herself until she was dizzy from lack of nourishment. She had been to every gym, every Weight Watcher's meeting, and had lost a thousand pounds in her lifetime, only to gain twice that amount back. Though she really did want to fit in and look the way everyone thought she should, it was much easier wished for than actually done.

Her co-workers never invited her to go along when they went to lunch, or when they went out for drinks after work. It was high school all over again until Sarah started working with Allison. They became fast friends, going almost everywhere together.

When Sarah discovered Allison didn't have much of a wardrobe, she dragged her to the mall to go shopping. She wasn't the least bit embarrassed to be seen with Allison, or by shopping at Lane Bryant's. Allison amassed quite a nice wardrobe over her two-year friendship with Sarah, and began to view herself differently. She lost forty pounds, and thanks to Sarah's friendship, and the new clothes, Allison felt better about herself.

With her head held high, her shoulders back, she had a new air of confidence, and an attitude.

Marie McGaha

Co-workers treated her differently. Men still didn't ask her to dance when she and Sarah went to the clubs together, but Allison told herself that was all right. One day she'd meet someone who would look past her outward appearance and see her for who she really was. Someone would fall in love with the person inside of her and she would marry and have children like she wanted to. Every night she went to bed alone and dreamed of the day a man would touch her and look at her with lust and love in his eyes. Being a twenty-three-year-old virgin was something she looked forward to changing as well. She wanted to be able to add to the girl gossip at work by telling tales of her own. Listening to the other women at work talk about their dating exploits only made Allison more self-conscious about herself.

Then she'd met Wesley. One day as she left the post office, Wesley came in with packages piled in his arms, and even though she tried to avoid him, he ran right into her, dropping the packages as he landed on the floor. As Allison bent down to help him, she tripped over one of the boxes and landed on top of him. Mortified when she heard his breath forced from his lungs by her weight, Allison didn't know what to say. Wesley only laughed and introduced himself as they lay on the floor with postal patrons skirting around the mess on the floor.

Allison helped picked up the packages and apologized profusely, but Wesley asked her to wait while he mailed his items, and then invited her for

Marie McGaha

coffee. They walked together down the block to a café where they talked for two hours over lattes and scones.

Not expecting to hear from him again, she gave him her number. He called her that night. She had never had a man pay attention to her before, at least not like this. So when he asked her out to dinner, she almost refused, thinking it was some ludicrous joke. Afterwards, knowing it was a mis-take, she let him come inside her apartment, and she lost her virginity that night. Allison had fallen in love with him, or at least she thought she was in love with him. Even if she wasn't, she told herself this might be her only shot to have a husband and all those babies she dreamed of. Wesley moved in with her the next weekend, and Allison was walking on air.

Allison couldn't wait to introduce Wesley to her best friend, Sarah. He and Sarah had started seeing each other almost immediately, and Allison had never felt so betrayed, so stupid, or *fat,* in her whole life. Thanks to the consolation she found in the tubs of Ben & Jerry's ice cream, she gained back twenty of the forty pounds she'd lost.

Well, that was it. Now she would accept the job she'd been offered in Biloxi, Mississippi. They could have each other. Chicago had never been her kind of town anyway. It was just too cold for a California girl anyway. Stomping to the kitchen, she picked up the phone while flipping through the Ro-

Marie McGaha

lodex. Dialing the number, she waited for someone to answer. She was about to hang up when a female voice finally answered.

"Hi, this is Allison Hamstead. Is Mr. Collins in please?"

"One moment, please. I'll transfer you."

"Thank you," Allison said and listened to music playing on the other end for at least ten minutes.

"May I help you?" It was a different female voice.

"Yes, I was on hold for Mister Collins."

"Whom may I say is calling?"

"Allison Hamstead."

"One moment, please."

Allison listened to the music for another ten minutes. She was beginning to think talking to the elusive Mr. Collins would prove impossible. Finally, a male voice came on the line.

"May I help you?"

"Mister Collins, this is Allison Hamstead. I'm calling to see if your job offer still stands. I'd like to accept if it does."

There was silence on the other end for a moment. "Job offer, Ms. Hamstead? I'm afraid I don't understand."

Allison blew her bangs out of her eyes, and tried not to sound impatient. "I applied online for the position of Executive Assistant Manager. You sent a reply about two weeks ago offering me the position."

Marie McGaha

"I'm going to put you on hold, Ms. Hamstead. I'll be right back."

Great, just great! Allison thought as she listened to the music again. If he didn't even remember offering her the job, it must have been filled already, and that would mean she was stuck where she was. She didn't want to go back to work and have to face Sarah every day. Not to mention all the awkward stares from other co-workers who were sure to know what happened.

"Ms. Hamstead, are you still there?"

"Yes, I'm here," she replied without much enthusiasm.

"I'm sorry for the mix up. The operator should have asked you which Mister Collins you wanted." He laughed. "I'm Stephen Collins. It's my brother, Jason, you want to speak with. If you will just hold for another few minutes, I'll try to transfer you. I'm not good with these phones, so if I hang up on you, please call back and ask for Jason Collins."

"Thank you. Thank you so much." She tried not to sound too excited, since she hadn't yet found out if the job was still available.

Stephen Collins chuckled. "You're welcome." She heard clicking on the other end before it rang again as the transfer successfully completed.

"Mister Collins's office, may I help you?"

"I hope so. I'm trying to reach Jason Collins, please."

"Whom may I say is calling?"

Marie McGaha

"Allison Hamstead."

"Jason Collins speaking," the male voice said and Allison thought he sounded remarkably like his brother.

"Hello, Mister Collins. This is Allison Hamstead. You offered me a job a couple of weeks ago. I'm calling to accept if the offer still stands."

"Hold on, let me pull your name. I'm sorry, but I had quite a few applicants and I don't remember one name from the next." She heard the keys on the computer keyboard clicking as he typed. "Okay, here we go. Mmm, hmm. Mmm, hmm," he said into the phone. "So you would like to accept the position, Ms. Hamstead?"

"Yes, sir, I would."

"When could you come down?"

"I could be there Monday if that's soon enough for you?"

"All right, Monday morning at eight then. Now I will tell you, Ms. Hamstead, this is a contingent hire. Since I am going solely on your resume, I will conduct an interview with you on Monday and you will spend the next thirty days working for me. That will be enough time for both of us to decide if the arrangement is going to work. If it does, we'll work up the contract for a permanent position, and if not, then you'll be free to leave. Is that acceptable to you, Ms. Hamstead?"

"Yes. Yes it is, Mister Collins. Thank you and I will see you on Monday."

Marie McGaha

"Eight a.m. sharp, Ms. Hamstead," he said curtly, and she heard the phone click off.

Looking at the phone in her hand for a moment, she frowned before hanging up. Another man had just called her an *arrangement*. She would have felt much better if the offer had been a permanent one from the beginning. What if he didn't like her and she wound up without a job? What if she really hated Mississippi or Mr. Collins? She had no family, no friends, nothing at all in Mississippi. Moving there would take most of what she'd managed to save, and she couldn't afford to keep her apartment in Chicago while she waited to see how this "arrangement" was going to work out. Besides, once she quit her job here, she couldn't come back in thirty days and announce she wanted it back.

Allison returned to the living room, sat on the sofa, and put her head between her knees.

"Okay, Allison," she said. "Pull yourself together, you have a lot to do." This was a huge step, she thought, but at least her heart wasn't on the line this time. If the job in Mississippi didn't work out, the only thing she'd lose was money, she knew she could always find another job.

After booking her flight for Saturday afternoon, she called her boss and quit her job, grabbed her luggage from the closet and began to pack. There was very little to take with her really. The apartment had come furnished, so she didn't have to worry about storing furniture and moving it to Missis-

Marie McGaha

sippi later. The few personal items she had would only take a few boxes that she could leave with a girl she'd tutored in college. She would ask Kim to mail the boxes to her when she found another apartment. That was, *if* she had another apartment.

Shaking that thought away, she knew she had to make a go of this job. She would also need a ride to the airport and someone to keep her car for her, so she picked up the phone and dialed Kim's number.

"Al, this is huge. I can't believe you're moving to Mississippi of all places. What language do they speak down there anyway?"

"Plain English, as in keeping me on after the thirty days are up, I hope. What on earth am I doing?"

"I don't know if I could do it. I'd be thinking all the time that I was going to be out of a job, with no place to go, the entire thirty days. I'd just be waiting for the ax to fall."

"Gee, thanks Kim. I feel so much better now," Allison said dryly.

"Sorry, Al. Can't you find another job here? You don't have to leave the state because of Wesley."

"It's not just that, Kim. I never did feel like Chicago was home. In the two years I've been here, it's never felt right. Ya know? I'm a California girl, born and raised by the ocean, and this just isn't the same."

Marie McGaha

"So why not go back to California?"

"I would if it wasn't so expensive. Gas out there is even higher than it is here. My cousin lives in a one bedroom apartment and pays over eleven-hundred dollars a month. I just can't afford that."

"Is it cheaper in Mississippi?"

"So I hear. Guess I'll find out. Hey, I gotta go. I've got some other things I have to do. I'll call you when I get down there, and let you know what I think about it. Who knows, it might work out."

"If it doesn't, you can come back here and stay with me until you get a job." Kim offered.

"Thanks, I appreciate it. We'll need to leave around one tomorrow, okay? My flight's at four. That should be enough time to get to the airport and get checked in."

"All right. I'll be ready," Kim assured her. She would be going to the airport with her so she could drive Allison's car back.

Going to the bank and closing her savings account, Allison left her checking account open to make sure everything cleared. She thought of going by and telling Wesley she was leaving town, then thought better of it. Why give him the satisfaction? Nothing good could come from seeing him or Sarah, and she knew they'd only think she was desperate and pathetic. Much the way she thought of herself at the moment. Making a quick turn, Allison went through the drive-thru of a fast food place and then went home to spend her last night in Chicago.

ONE GOOD MAN

Marie McGaha

~ * ~

Allison stood in line at the airport pulling her carry-on bag behind her, and a latte in the other hand. Her laptop was in the carry-on. She thought she would update her resume during the flight, just in case. Placing her things on the conveyer belt, she removed her watch and earrings before walking through the metal detector. She waited for what seemed like an eternity, but finally boarded the plane and settled into her seat with her laptop and a paperback novel.

The flight to Mississippi was uneventful, and when she landed at the Gulfport/Biloxi airport, she retrieved her luggage at baggage claim, and went outside to hail a cab. The January air was warm and smelled of saltwater. Inhaling deeply, Allison grinned. You didn't get that in Chicago. She told the driver to take her to the Golden Lady Casino. Settling back in the seat, she enjoyed the ride along the Gulf Coast.

Marie McGaha

~ Two ~

"May I help you?" The desk clerk asked as Allison set her purse on the counter.

"Yes. I need a room, please."

The clerk laid a card and pen on the counter. "Fill this out please."

Allison picked up the pen and began filling out the card.

"I don't know how many nights I'll need just yet," she told the clerk. "I'll start working for Mr. Jason Collins on Monday, but I don't know how long it will take me to find an apartment."

"Oh, you're Ms. Hamstead?"

"Yes, but call me Allison. Or Al, as most of my friends do," she said with a friendly grin offering her hand.

The man shook it and said, "I'm Leonard. Mr. Collins arranged for your accommodations for the next month. You'll be staying in room 18A. It's on the first floor, aft." He handed her a key card.

"Aft?" Allison looked at him as she took the key.

"Since the casino is a ship, we use nautical terms here. You may as well learn them quickly. Cap'n Collins will have a fit if he hears you use a different term." Leonard rolled his eyes.

"Cap'n Collins?"

"Yeah, you'll be working for Jason Collins, but his father, Nelson, is the one who owns the casino,

Marie McGaha

and everyone calls him Captain. Stephen is the first mate."

Making sure no one else was within earshot, he leaned over the counter, and in a conspiratorial tone told her, "Like I said, he insists we use nautical terms. Stephen is the CEO here and Jason is the VP, but don't let anyone know I called them that. If it gets back to the Cap'n, he'll make me walk the plank."

"All righty then." Allison smiled and shook her head. She was beginning to think she'd walked into the middle of the Twilight Zone.

"Here." He laid a map of the casino on the counter. "We're right here." He pointed with a pen. "You'll go through this set of doors here at the end of the counter, make a right down the hallway, and just keep going until you come to the next set of double doors. Go through them, and then just look for the numbers on the doors. It'll be on the right-hand side."

"Thank you, Leonard. It was nice meeting you."

"Nice to meet you too, Al. I'm going to call up and let Jason know you're here, but I'll give you an hour or so to settle in and freshen up. I will have someone bring your luggage."

"Thanks." She smiled at him, as she headed for the door at the end of the desk. Pulling her carry-on behind her, she walked down the corridor until she finally came to a set of double doors and pushed

Marie McGaha

them open. Continuing down the hall, she watched the numbers until she came to her room. As she inserted the key card, opened the door, and entered the room, she noticed that, even though it wasn't very large, it looked comfortable.

Crossing the deep-sea blue carpet, she opened the matching curtains and found she had a view of the gulf. Smiling, she opened one window and breathed deeply of the salt air. She turned back to the room and noticed the bed was covered with a blue and white bedspread decorated with sailing ships. The lampshades were also decorated with ships and seashells adorning the base. She laughed and shook her head. Captain Collins certainly took his fantasy to great lengths.

Allison set her laptop on the desk, emptied everything from her carry-on, and put it on the closet shelf next to the bathroom. Sitting down, she booted her computer. She'd seen Johnny Depp in *Pirates of the Caribbean,* all three movies in fact, so she knew port meant left and starboard meant right, but that was the extent of her nautical knowledge. The fact that she had been raised less than a mile from the ocean didn't mean she'd been on a boat before. *Oops, ship I mean!* She thought and chuckled.

Deep into a Google search when the phone rang, Allison jumped and laughed as she went to answer it.

"Hello?"

Marie McGaha

"Allison, this is Jason Collins. I know we said we'd meet on Monday morning, but I've been forced to work this weekend. So I thought perhaps you could join me for supper and we can get the interview out of the way now."

"Of course, sir. When would you like to meet?"

"How about thirty minutes?"

"Fine. I'll see you then."

"Just tell the hostess who you are, and she'll bring you to my table," he instructed just before he clicked off. Allison looked at the phone and thought he had a bad habit of hanging up without saying good-bye.

Shutting down the computer, she went into the bathroom, stripped out of her clothing, and took a quick shower. Stepping out of the shower, and wrapping a towel around her dripping body, Allison heard a knock. She stepped out to the door and peered thru the peephole, to see a bellhop with her luggage.

"Just leave it right there!" *About time.*

Watching through the peephole until the man left, she opened the door and dragged her suitcases into the room. She heaved them over onto the bed and unzipped the lids. Choosing a pair of cream-colored linen slacks, with a sleeveless top a couple of shades darker than the slacks and buttoned up the front, she decided that she wanted to appear businesslike, yet casual. Also, she wanted to appear

Marie McGaha

thin. Allison sighed, knowing that nothing she wore would help in that area. She slipped on a pair of flats and looked in the mirror. *Well it is better than being short and fat.*

In the bathroom, she combed out her wet hair, dried it with the built-in blow dryer, and put on her make-up. Looking at herself again in the full-length mirror on the closet door, she shrugged. *Could be worse.* Grabbing her purse and key-card, Allison headed for the dining room.

~ * ~

Jason Collins had been sitting at his table in the dining room observing the guests coming and going at the seafood buffet. They were the lifeblood of the casino. He, his brother, and their father, made sure their guests had every amenity in their rooms and the finest food made by the best chefs they could find. Occasionally, he glanced toward the entrance to see if Tracey, the hostess this evening, was escorting his dinner guest.

A stickler for punctuality, Jason could not abide tardiness. It was one of the reasons he'd invited Allison to dinner. He wanted to see what thirty minutes meant to her. To some people it could mean anytime from fifteen minutes to forty-five minutes, to others it would mean thirty minutes to an hour. To Jason, it meant thirty minutes exactly, and while he'd not care if she were five minutes early, arriving five minutes late would not go in her favor.

Marie McGaha

When he looked up again, he saw Tracey coming toward him with a young woman beside her. Glancing at his watch, he noticed the time was six twenty-nine. Smiling, he stood as she reached the table and extended his hand.

"Ms. Hamstead?"

"Yes, but please call me Allison, or Al. Either way is fine with me," she said with a friendly smile. Taking his proffered hand, she gripped it tightly. He liked that, too.

"Please, have a seat." He thanked Tracey as he took his seat.

"You have a lovely place, Mister Collins." Allison felt nervous and hoped it didn't show as she slid into the booth. Her large body fit snuggly between the table and the seat back.

"Thank you. I'm glad you could come at such short notice."

"I didn't have much on my social schedule." She replied, laughing lightly, hoping she didn't sound as nervous as she felt.

"Shall we order from the menu, or would you prefer the buffet?"

"I'd like to see a menu. The buffet looks tempting, but I think it would be too distracting if I were jumping up and down to fill my plate. Besides, with a meal from the menu, I'll be limited to the amount I can eat, and you won't see what a chowhound I can be." As always, she tried to make light

Marie McGaha

of her size, and somehow, being the one to bring it
up, seemed to ease the tension she felt.

He smiled. "I see we both have the same
problem then." He waved at one of the waitresses,
who hurried over with two menus.

"Everything looks so good. What do you recommend, Mister Collins?"

"First, I recommend that you start calling me
Jason," he said and looked at her over the top of the
menu. "And if you like Italian, the pasta here is ex-
cellent."

"Wonderful. I'll have the ravioli," Allison told
the waitress and laid her menu aside.

"I'll have the same, and bring me another
whiskey sour." Jason drained his glass. "Allison,
what do you drink?"

"A red appletini is fine for me, thank you."

"Tell me about yourself," Jason said when the
waitress walked away.

She frowned slightly, then smiled just as
quickly, and said, "I hate that question. It always
puts me on the spot and I don't know what to say."

"That's the point of the question."

"I don't have a long resume, Mister Collins,
but I'm good at what I do. My mother worked two
jobs to support us, and I was the one who took care
of the bills and managed her income so we had what
we needed, with some left over for the things we
wanted. She managed to put me through college and

Marie McGaha

I went to work for Markham Brothers in L.A. before being transferred to Chicago.

"I've lived in Chicago for the past two years, working for Markham Brothers in the windy city." She smiled.

"And now you want to work in a casino?"

"Not really. I wanted to live by the ocean again, and I wanted to be some place with warmer winters. I also wanted my salary to equal the cost of living. It didn't in either California or Chicago. But working in a casino will give me the type of experience I would never get at Markham's. The faster pace will add an element of excitement, and I tend to work better when there's a little pressure."

"I have to tell you Allison, you speak honestly and straight forward. I like that. Now, it can get very hectic around here, especially during peak season. It's busy year round of course, but during the vacation season, it can be a mad house. My wife, Shelly, works here as well, and you'll get to know her. She's home with the kids right now, but she'll be here on Monday, and I'll introduce you. Do you have children?"

"No," she said shaking her head. "I've never married."

"We don't allow dating between employees here, Allison, or between the employees and guests. We don't allow our guests to harass the employees either, so if anyone gets too fresh, don't hesitate to tell someone and we'll take care of it. You will have

Marie McGaha

your own office on the second floor, but as part of the management team, you will be expected to spend time on the casino floor. The Captain is big on managers being seen, setting an example by doing, and not just by telling others what to do."

Allison nodded.

"I almost forgot to thank you for my room. I didn't expect you to provide one for me."

"You're welcome. We thought that since you were here for a thirty-day probationary period, there was no reason for you to have to worry about finding a place to live. If it works out for everyone involved, you can find a place when the thirty days is up."

"Thank you, I appreciate it."

Jason looked up as a man approached the table. "I thought you had gone home."

"I was just on my way out, so I thought I'd stop by and meet your new assistant."

"Stephen Collins, I would like to introduce Allison Hamstead. Allison, this is the First Mate, and my brother, Stephen."

"Nice to meet you, Big Al," Stephen said with a grin, shaking her hand. Forcing Jason to move over, he sat in the booth with them.

"We spoke briefly on the phone," she told him. "But it's nice meeting you too... Stevie." She shortened his name deliberately. He only raised a brow, but Jason chuckled.

Marie McGaha

"I think she's already got your number there big brother," Jason laughed, and the waitress set dinner and drinks on the table.

The waitress looked at Stephen and grinned. "You want anything, Stephen?"

He grinned back and took a long, slow look up and down.

"Not right now, Heather," he drawled, "but thanks for askin'."

"Anytime," Heather said as she wiggled away.

Jason shot his brother a stern look.

"You shouldn't be flirting with the waitresses in front of Allison, she'll get the wrong impression."

"Oh, I don't think I've got the wrong impression about your brother at all," Allison commented, not sparing Stephen another glance.

Stephen laughed out loud and Jason grinned.

"Allison, I think you're going to be around here for quite a while. There aren't many females who can resist my brother's charms." Taking a bite of pasta, he muttered loudly enough for Stephen to hear, "Whatever they may be."

"Come on Jase," Stephen said as he elbowed his brother. "You know it's harmless, I never let it go past the flirting stage with the waitresses."

"Only because Captain would kill you if you did."

"Be that as it may, I still keep my hands to myself." He shot Allison a wink, finished his drink, and set the empty glass on the table.

Marie McGaha

"Allison, it was nice meeting you. I hope you'll decide to stay on in spite of your low opinion of me."

"Thank you, but I don't have a low opinion of you." She smiled innocently, and looked up at him as he stood.

"Really?" He grinned wolfishly down at her.

"Really. To have a low opinion of you would indicate that I have put forth the effort to care enough to *have* an opinion of you. Rest assured that I do not." She went back to her ravioli.

"Ouch!" Stephen laughed as he walked away.

"Congratulations, Allison. You are the first woman to ever work here that didn't fall all over herself to get my brother to notice her," Jason told her with a chuckle.

"I'm glad I didn't offend you, Jason. Although I should have thought before I said anything. Men like that just sit wrong with me."

"Tell me what kind of man you think my brother is," Jason said as he wiped his plate with a piece of buttered sourdough bread.

"You know, he's the charming type that thinks he's every woman's dream, and all he has to do is snap his fingers for her panties to fall off." She looked up at Jason as she suddenly realized what she'd said. "Oh my goodness, I am *so* sorry."

Jason laughed out loud. "Don't worry about it. You really do know my brother."

Marie McGaha

Allison felt the heat in her cheeks and shook her head, then downed the last of her martini. She looked up at him and smiled wryly. "Now if you'd just help me get my foot out of my mouth, I'd be forever grateful."

"No, I think I like you with your foot right where it is. You just continue being that honest and outspoken in everything around here, and you'll do well.

"My brother is a good businessman, I'll give him that, and as CEO around here, I couldn't ask for anyone better. As far as his personal life goes, he's the kind of man that gives the rest of us a bad name. I love him dearly, don't get me wrong, but he goes through women faster than he goes through clean socks.

"As a matter of fact, when I first started dating my wife, she and I had gone to the movies one Saturday afternoon. I had just gotten my driver's license, so I wasn't allowed to drive at night," Jason confided. "Anyway, we came back to the house and were sitting in the living room drinking a Coke and talking, when Stephen came home. He sat down with us, and when I went to the bathroom, he put his arm around her and asked her out. And he was serious."

"So what happened?"

"Shelly told me what he did as soon as I got back, and all Stephen did was laugh and say that I couldn't blame him for trying. I gave him a black eye

Marie McGaha

and Captain tanned both of us." Jason laughed at the memory.

"We're just ten months apart, he being the eldest, but throughout our lives, Captain has treated us the same. No matter what happened, if one of us did something wrong, we both got into trouble. If one of us did something good, we were both rewarded."

"That hardly seems fair," Allison commented.

"We didn't think so at the time either, but it taught us the 'all for one and one for all' concept. Now we're the best of friends and work well together." He glanced at his watch. "I've kept you long enough, Allison. My wife is going to kill me for being so late tonight. You'll meet her and Captain on Monday.

"Get some sleep and spend tomorrow touring the area. I think you'll like it. The home of Jefferson Davis is here, he was the first, and only, president of the confederate states. Pascagoula isn't that far of a drive, and New Orleans is only ninety miles if you want to see Bourbon Street or the Garden District. Lots of history found in the south."

"Thanks. You should be working for the visitor's bureau," she said with a laugh.

Jason smiled. "Come on, I'll walk you to the front desk."

~ * ~

Stephen Collins drove the greatest classic car ever made, at least in his opinion: a '69 Ford Mus-

Marie McGaha

tang Boss 429, painted flat black, with chrome trim, and a spoiler on the back. He took better care of that car than anything else he owned. He'd worked long and hard to be able to afford it, and then worked harder and longer to have it cherried out. It was his pride and joy, and a babe magnet—and in Biloxi, there was never a shortage of babes. They came in droves during spring break and all summer long. The Gulf Coast was his own personal playground, and he took advantage of the perks.

It wasn't as if he didn't want a permanent relationship—someday. He did, but today wasn't that day. His brother had married right out of high school and had three children in the first three years of the marriage. But it worked for Jason and Shelly, and he knew it would work for him as well. One day in the very distant future, that is. He was only twenty-eight years old, and there was no way he was going to be tied down yet.

Besides, when he met the woman he would marry, it would be forever. He wasn't going to go through wives like his father had, or be divorced within the first five years, like so many of his friends from college. Nope, when Stephen married, it would be forever the first time around, and if he wasn't absolutely sure about that, he wasn't going to do it.

He swung the Mustang into the garage of his house and the overhead door slowly shut behind him. Inside, he pushed the button on his answering machine and grinned when he heard Lisa's voice. She

Marie McGaha

had just turned twenty-one, and they'd met the night before at one of the clubs where she had been celebrating her birthday. He had a present for her all right, but she had been with friends and wouldn't leave them to go with him, at least not then. However, she was his tonight. She lived in Oklahoma and would be leaving in the morning, so that made her the perfect woman as far as Stephen was concerned. He liked women who knew the meaning of *hit the highway.*

Taking the stairs two at a time, he went into his bedroom, stripped down, went into the bathroom and stepped into the shower. He thought about his brother's new assistant and wondered about her attitude toward him. Women found him attractive, *all* women, and he couldn't figure out why she disliked him so much. Maybe she just hated men in general. Some women were like that, they'd been hurt by someone and took it out on all men.

Her face was pretty, and he liked the dark honey color of her hair, and her long lashes set off her beautiful jade-colored eyes. Maybe her face was a little too round, but the dimples in her cheeks were cute. He could tell she wore some make-up, but she managed to keep her look natural. Though he'd yet to see her standing, he was sure she was tall. She was just a big girl all around. However, she didn't seem to like him at all.

Suddenly, it dawned on him, his mouth. He'd called her "Big Al". *What an idiot!* Though not in-

Marie McGaha

tended as a reference to her size, he suddenly realized she must have taken his remark that way. He just didn't always think before he spoke, and now he'd inadvertently insulted a new employee. There had to be a way to make it up to her so she'd like him. She had to, all women loved him, and he couldn't imagine this one being any different.

That was a completely foreign concept to him, but he grinned anyway. Not that he was arrogant, well, okay, so he was arrogant, but women liked him. They liked him a lot. Even when he told them there was no future with him. He never led a woman on. He made sure they knew a date was just a date, or a one-night stand, or a weekend, whatever the situation, he was completely honest.

Learning his lesson a long time ago, he knew that honesty was always the best way to handle any situation. It presented less fuss and mess in the end. And he definitely didn't like a mess. But what would it take to make Allison like him? That question bothered him the rest of the night.

Later on, as he danced with his date, he still couldn't get his mind off of Allison, and even when he pulled Lisa close and kissed her passionately, Allison was the picture he saw in his mind. He whispered in Lisa's ear, inviting her back to his townhouse. She smiled up at him and declined. What was going on here? Two women in the same day *not* wanting him was enough to keep him up the rest of the night—and not in a good way.

Marie McGaha

~ Three ~

Monday morning, Allison rose early, showered and chose her blue pinstriped suit to wear for her meeting with Jason and the rest of the Collins family. Taking a deep breath, she tried to calm her nervousness about meeting the Captain. Sliding her feet into a pair of navy flats, Allison looked herself over in the mirror. The pin-stripe pattern made her appear thinner, or at least she thought so, and she hoped it made her breasts look smaller as well. Having thought often of spending the money on a breast reduction right along with the gastric by-pass surgery, she could almost convince herself to take the drastic measures. Frowning into the mirror, she wasn't what she would call happy with her appearance, but she was satisfied. Grabbing her navy bag and briefcase, she left the room.

The office door read "J. Collins-Vice President," and Allison paused long enough to take a deep, calming breath before opening the door. The room was done in red from the carpets to the draperies, to the suit worn by the woman behind the mahogany desk. The secretary looked up briefly and scanned Allison the way women do one another—just a quick appraisal that neither indicated approval nor disapproval.

"Allison Hamstead?"

"Yes." Allison hoped she didn't appear as nervous as she felt.

Marie McGaha

"I'm Ellen, Mister Collins' secretary. Right this way," the woman said, rising from her chair. Allison followed her down a short hallway to the conference room. Holding the door open, she motioned for Allison to enter. "You'll do fine," she whispered as Allison passed. Allison flashed a quick smile and walked into the meeting.

The room reminded her of King Arthur and the Knights of the Round Table. In the center of the room was a round oak table with all the seats occupied except for one between Jason Collins and a man who looked much like him, only older.

"Allison. You're right on time. Come on in." Jason rose from his chair. So did the man sitting next to him.

"I want you to meet the man who makes all of this possible, my father, Nelson, otherwise known as Captain." Jason winked slyly at her and then gestured to a woman sitting next to him. "And this beauty is my wife, Shelly. You remember my brother, Stephen, I'm sure. This is Sam," Jason continued, ignoring his brother's obvious attempt to flirt with Allison.

"He's head of security and you'll be seeing him after the meeting for fingerprinting and a security check. And this is Janet. She'll be your personal secretary. If you need anything or have questions, ask her. If she doesn't have an answer, there isn't one," Jason said with a smile as he finished the introductions.

Marie McGaha

"Hello." Allison looked at each person so she would remember every name and the face it belonged to. This was a little trick she'd learned in college that had served her well, especially in business situations where she met several new people on a daily basis and was expected to know them later. "I'm very happy to be here, and to meet all of you."

"Here Allison, take this chair," Captain offered.

"Thank you," Allison said and sat down between her boss and his father.

The meeting took more than two hours and Allison felt as if the CIA had given her the third degree. When it was over, Janet and Sam escorted her to the security office where she was fingerprinted and photographed.

"It's for our own peace of mind," Sam explained while rolling her fingers on the black inkpad. When he was finished, Allison followed Janet to her office, which was also done in red like Jason's, and had the same dark mahogany furniture.

"They're all done this way. Very male." Janet smiled. "And don't let Captain's gruffness get to you. He's really a teddy bear, but he likes his employees to do things right, of course, and he won't tolerate anyone breaking his rules. Aside from that, the man is the sweetest person you'll ever meet.

"He's also a flirt, but don't take that seriously either. He's had four wives and there's no sign of number five—yet, but everyone is sure there will be.

Marie McGaha

And you'd think that at his age, he'd be settling into old age and calming down, since he's nearly seventy. Though don't dare say I told you that, he'll skin me.

"This is my desk here in the front office," Janet continued without so much as taking a breath. "And if you'll follow me down here," she said as she led Allison down the hallway and pushed open a door. "This is your office. If you find you need anything, just let me know and I'll put in an order for it. The Captain doesn't mind any of us having what we need to be more efficient, but we do have to put in a purchase order that requires five copies.

"I'll write it up for you and then you'll sign it, and I'll file one of the copies. The other copies go to Captain, Jason and Stephen, and the fifth goes to the ordering clerk. Captain insists that it's done that way so there's no skimming off the top. He runs a tight ship," she laughed, "if you'll excuse the expression. Do you drink coffee?"

"Yes, but I'd like to bring in my cappuccino machine."

"Oh, don't worry about that. For coffee or cappuccino, or any kind of drink, just dial one-seven on the phone. That'll get you to the kitchen. Ask for Lynette. Tell her who you are, and she'll have one sent up to you. The same goes for lunch if you decide to work through, or don't want to go out.

"Management gets one free meal a day, lunch or dinner, and your coffee is free. Mister Collins takes good care of his employees. Well, all three of

Marie McGaha

them do, but I'm kind of partial to Jason and his wife."

"He seems very nice. Everyone does. I had dinner with Jason on Saturday night and he was very warm," Allison said. "I think I'd like to take a tour of the ship now, kind of get a feel for everything, get my bearings, you know?"

"Sure. Do you want me to go with you?"

"No, that's all right. I don't want to keep you from your work. Plus, I'll be able to get a feel for things on my own. If I have questions, and I know I will," she said with a laugh, "I'll hit you up for answers when I get back."

~ * ~

She liked the casino. It vibrated and pulsed like a living being with an energy and spirit of its own. People came and went, bells and whistles sounded as if change were clanging into the bins when someone won, although with new technology, even slot machines didn't give back real money, but a voucher redeemable at the counter. It still seemed as if everyone had a lot of fun, and even small wins were reason for hoots and hollers from the people nearby.

They were dressed in shorts, shirts and flip-flops, summer dresses, and khaki slacks and polo shirts. They were young, middle aged, and old. Age didn't seem to have a bearing on the conversations they had with one another. No matter who won, everyone else was excited and happy about it, and when someone lost, everyone sympathized as well.

Allison smiled and nodded to various people as she walked through the casino, observing everything that went on. She'd been in Indian casinos a few times, but wasn't much of a gambler. Once when she, Kim, and Sarah had gone together for a weekend gambling spree, Allison had taken a hundred dollars to gamble away, which was half of what the other girls took. When they'd finished gambling and everyone else was broke, Allison still had seventy-five dollars of her gambling money left, and not because she'd won, but because when she lost the first twenty-five, she quit.

"Nope, definitely not a gambler," she muttered.

"What?"

Allison started and turned so quickly she nearly lost her balance. "Oh, nothing. Just checking out everything."

"So what do you think?" Stephen Collins fell into step beside her.

Looking at him, she answered, "It's really wonderful. Not at all what I thought it would be."

"What were you expecting?"

"I don't really know. I've only been to a couple of Indian casinos and they were nothing like this."

"You've never been to Las Vegas or Atlantic City?"

Marie McGaha

Allison shook her head.

"You're kidding?"

"Don't sound so shocked. I hear there are people who manage their whole lives without ever going to either place."

"Yeah, but they regret it after they die," he said with a grin. He reminded her of a very naughty little boy.

Laughing with him, she said, "Then I guess I'll have to make a special trip one day just so I don't regret it after I die. Although, I'm not much of a gambler. I work too hard for my money to throw it away on games of chance."

He shoved his hands deep in his pockets. "These people all work hard for their money too, yet, here they are, poking it into machines and laying it down for one roll of the dice. And when they get home, they have stories to tell their friends of how close they came to winning the big one."

"What about the ones who spend their kid's college money, or the mortgage payment, on that roll of the dice?"

He shrugged. "It happens, I won't try and pretend it doesn't, but that's life. The ones that have a problem with gambling have problems elsewhere too. We aren't babysitters. This is adult fun, and hopefully everyone here will conduct themselves accordingly, and go home feeling good about themselves."

Marie McGaha

"Well, I should get back upstairs. I told Janet that I'd go over some things when I got back. I still have to learn the ropes around here."

"Janet will be able to teach them to you. She probably knows this place as well as my father does. Have a good day, Allison." He grinned and she felt her heart leap.

"You too," she muttered and turned away, trying not to run from him.

Allison pushed the button on the elevator and wished it would hurry. She did not want Stephen sharing such a small space with her, even if it was for only two floors. There was simply too much of him for her to be trapped within the small space of an elevator. And he was too handsome for her taste. She'd learned her lesson with good-looking men. Wesley was extremely attractive, but beside Stephen, he was a frog in designer suits.

Stephen Collins' dark hair was worn too long with a distracting lock that kept falling down onto his brow. His black eyes flashed with mischievous humor. His nose was straight, his cheekbones high, and his lips were perfect for kissing. *Oh, Allison, stop thinking about him!*

But, of course, when one tried to stop thinking about something, it was the only thing that came to mind. One really couldn't stop thinking about something without actually thinking about it in the first place, could one? She wrinkled her nose as she puzzled over that for a moment.

ONE GOOD MAN

Marie McGaha

His shoulders were certainly broad, but she knew he got that from his father. Even for a man of nearly seventy, Allison thought Captain was still very attractive, and probably looked a lot like Stephen when he was younger. Stephen had muscular arms too, she'd observed, and his rear, well, a girl had to look at that—you could bounce quarters off it. His stomach was flat and he walked with a confident swagger. And why wouldn't a man who looked like that be confident? Every woman in the free world would probably fall all over herself to have him cast that wicked smile of his her way.

Except me, that is, she thought. Nope, she wouldn't look at him twice, even if he were the last man on earth. Men who looked like that didn't notice women like Allison, at least they didn't notice them for the purpose of dating or falling in love. Besides, Allison's heart had been broken all it was going to be. Learning her lessons quickly, so they wouldn't have to be repeated, Allison thought she must have gotten that from her mother. Allison's father had broken her mother's heart, and Trudy Hamstead had protected hers from being broken again for over twenty-three years.

Allison sighed as she stepped onto the elevator and pushed the button. It occurred to her as the elevator began to go up, that it was only going one floor, and it would have been much quicker to use the stairs. She'd just gotten so used to going to work on the nineteenth floor in Chicago, she hadn't even

47

considered that option. From now on, she thought, she'd opt for the exercise and climb instead of ride. Here she could even walk on the beach the way she used to do in California. Maybe she could start riding a bike for exercise, or by kissing Stephen Collins.

"Oh my! Where did that come from?" Allison said without realizing it, just as the elevator door opened.

"Is there a problem?" Captain asked.

"Oh, no sir. I had just... just thought of something I forgot to do." Allison knew she was blushing furiously.

Captain merely smiled and Allison found herself thinking what a handsome man he was while he surveyed her with those dark eyes of his. And she knew exactly where Stephen had gotten that mischievous grin.

"So you were below decks were you? What do you think of our little establishment?"

"I think it's wonderful." She grinned broadly, showing her dimples.

"Come with me, young lady." He offered his arm and Allison slipped her hand through. They stepped back onto the elevator and he pushed the button labeled '5'. "I want to show you the rest of the ship." Stepping off on the fifth floor, they were outside on the observation deck. The town of Biloxi sprawled out inland, with the Gulf of Mexico behind them. It was a beautiful sight.

Marie McGaha

"I was raised by the ocean," she told him. "I haven't been home in two years and I've missed it so much. I'll like living by the ocean again."

"What about your parents? Haven't you even been home to visit them?"

"There's only my mother. I'm an only child and my mother never remarried after my father left us."

"Do you see your father?"

"No, I've never even met him. He left before I was born, and we never heard from him again."

Smiling at the woman on his arm as they walked across the deck to the railing, he said, "I think you're going to be a valuable asset around here Allison."

"Thank you, Captain. I appreciate that coming from you," Allison said, dragging her gaze away from the view.

"I'm a businessman Allison, and I recognize ambition, and I recognize what's good for my business. You have ambition. I'm glad my son was able to recognize that as well, and hired you."

"Thank you." She smiled shyly.

"Come on. Let me show you the rest of the ship."

Marie McGaha

~ Four ~

Three weeks had passed when Captain ordered Allison to take a day off. The work hours were
long and she worked hard. Going to bed exhausted
every night, she woke every morning excited about
being there. She'd become friends with Shelly Collins and was in love with Shelly's three children. She
also felt a deep affection for the Captain. They had
developed a very father-daughter sort of relationship, something she had never had with any man in
her life, and she liked the way it felt. They ate lunch
together often, and when she was working too hard,
he came by to make her take walks on the beach
with him. Furthermore, she had managed to avoid
Stephen much of the time. When she had to speak
with him personally, she was all business, and never
gave him the slightest indication she had any inter-
est in him.

After sleeping in, she made her way to the
beach. For nearly an hour, she walked along the
shoreline before turning around and walking back.
Sitting with her feet buried in the sand, she watched
gulls dive in the sea and children play in the water.
Glad she'd come to the south, she wanted to stay,
and hoped that when her thirty days were up, she'd
be asked to stay on permanently. The town of Biloxi
was wonderful, but she really loved Gulfport, which
felt like home for some reason. She'd found a restaurant there called the *White Cap* that served some

Marie McGaha

of the best seafood she'd ever eaten. The south was wonderful, and she liked the people, their accents and their genuine hospitality. Allison was surprised by how many had been born and raised right there in Mississippi, although there were more and more people moving in from out of state all the time.

As she lay back on her towel, a shadow fell across her. She opened one eye to see Stephen standing over her, grinning. "You're blocking my sun," she said and shut her eye.

"Mind if I join you?"

"Yes, I do mind."

"Thanks."

Turning toward him, she again opened one eye and frowned as she discovered he had removed his shirt and spread his towel beside her.

"There's a lot of beach here you know, you could pick another spot."

"Yeah, but I like this one."

"You're just trying to make me mad."

"Now why would I do that?"

"Because you act like a twelve year old and teasing girls is what twelve year olds do."

"Yeah, but my toys are much bigger and go a lot faster," he smirked.

She rolled her eyes and went back to sunning herself in silence. Stephen didn't speak for a long time either, which she thought was a blessing and probably too good to last long. She was right.

"Have dinner with me."

Marie McGaha

"Why?"

"Why not?"

"Because it's fraternizing and your father doesn't allow it."

"Not true. We're just two colleagues having dinner together. The fraternizing rule only applies between management and underlings. He's afraid an employee would feel their position would be threatened if they refused a date with management."

"Or perhaps he just didn't want you dating the entire staff."

He laughed. "That's a possibility."

"You're shameless."

"So I've been told."

"I'm not having dinner with you."

"I'll pick you up at seven."

"Look, Stephen, you don't have to do this." She sat up and looked at him squarely.

"Do what?" He asked, almost managing to look innocent.

"All of this..."she waved one arm, "this flirting you seem to be doing with me. I'm not exactly your type."

"What do you mean my type? That's pretty judgmental and shallow of you." He grinned at her again.

"And if anyone would know about shallow, it would be you, now wouldn't it?" She said rather tersely. "Just stop it."

ONE GOOD MAN

Marie McGaha

"Allison... "Stephen watched as she picked up her things and began making her way toward the casino. He blew out a breath and shook his head.

~ * ~

The phone rang just as Allison entered her room. "Hello," she said, pushing her hair back from her face.

"Have you eaten yet?" Captain asked her.

"No, sir," she said, grinning at the sound of his rough voice.

"Then come on down to the dining room around seven and have supper with me. We're eating in the banquet hall."

"I'll be there," she told him.

"That's a good girl," he replied and clicked off.

Allison smiled and hung up. She took a long shower, dressed casually, and a few minutes before seven she went to the banquet hall in the rear of the dining room. When she opened the door and walked in, she found the whole family waiting for her. Grinning, Captain brought her to a chair beside him, and kissed her cheek as she sat.

"I didn't realize everyone would be here, but this is so nice."

Growing up as an only child, Allison had never experienced this type of atmosphere with family all crowded around the table noisily trying to shout over everyone else in order to be heard. She loved it. Shelly and Jason sat on the other side of Captain and

Marie McGaha

next to them were their three children. Janet, whom Allison had found out was actually a cousin to Captain, was also present. The only one missing was Stephen. Allison thought perhaps he'd run into a woman on the beach and had taken off with her. She'd never actually seen Stephen with a woman, but his reputation preceded him, and his attitude irritated her.

She was to be even more irritated.

"Sorry I'm late," Stephen, said as he entered the room and took the empty chair next to Allison. "See," he said in a low voice leaning into her. "I told you you'd be having dinner with me." She ignored him and looked away. He chuckled to himself.

"Well, now that we're all here," Captain said and everyone quieted down. "Allison, we are having dinner tonight to celebrate your first month with us."

"Thank you, but it's only been three weeks."

"Close enough for us, darlin'." He smiled affectionately at her. "We are all impressed by the way you've come in here and taken to your job like you've done it all your life. We also think that it's not necessary to keep you waiting another week before we tell you that you are now a permanent employee here. Congratulations!" He held up his glass and everyone followed suit. "To Allison," he said and touched his lifted glass to hers, which was followed by clinking all around the table.

Marie McGaha

Stephen turned to Allison. "Aren't you going to allow me to toast you as well?" Reluctantly, she held up her glass and he touched his to hers. "Welcome aboard, Allison."

"Thank you," she said.

His dark eyes weren't teasing or mocking her now, and looking into them made her breath catch in her throat. She looked quickly away and drained her glass. The rest of the evening went smoothly, as long as Allison avoided looking directly at Stephen. It was like trying to avoid looking at the moon when it was full and hanging low, or a sunset when it washed the sky in hues of orange, pink, and red.

And she could actually feel his gaze upon her. His eyes seemed to burn into her, seemed to call to her, daring her to look his way. Instead, she concentrated paying attention to the conversation with the others at the table. Relieved when dinner was over, so she could escape to her room, Allison wanted nothing more than to call her mother.

Lying on the bed, a bit giddy from the champagne and the news she was there to stay, she knew it was nearly ten in California, and her mother would already be in bed, since she rose at five every morning. She'd call her tomorrow. She closed her eyes to go to sleep since she too, had an early morning. All she could see in her mind was Stephen, and she could still smell his scent in her nostrils. She tossed the blankets back and turned over.

~ * ~

Marie McGaha

Stephen was beside her, massaging her neck muscles in such a delicious way. She could have lay there all night and enjoyed his massaged. But then he kissed the back of her neck, and that was even better than the massage. "Oh, how wonderful," she sighed.

No, no, no! She reached for him, but he slipped away. "Stephen," she called as the alarm went off and *John Boy And Billy In The Morning* boomed over the radio. Allison jumped at the intrusion and hit the off button. She looked around, momentarily confused as the dream came rushing to mind.

What is wrong with you? she admonished herself, and stumbled into the bathroom. The shower ran hot over her head and body, and she was thankful it had a massaging head for her aching head. *Why did I drink so much?* She asked while washing her hair. She felt somewhat better when she dried off and dressed. Dialing the number to the kitchen, she ordered two triple lattes and told the voice on the phone to have them taken to her office as quickly as possible.

The bright lights of the main lobby assaulted her and she blinked several times before walking to the stairs and climbing them to the second floor. Halfway up she thought it might have been a better idea to use the elevator this morning. Holding her head with one hand, she finally made it to her desk.

Marie McGaha

A few minutes later, the coffee arrived and Allison swore it was the best she'd ever tasted.

"Not feeling so good this morning?" Stephen walked into her office.

"Go away," she mumbled and lowered her forehead to her arm on the desk.

He laughed. "You didn't even drink very much. I didn't realize you were such a light weight."

"Get out," came the muffled reply.

"Hey, I brought you some aspirin and coffee." He crossed the room and put a hand gently on her arm, then knelt down beside her.

"Come on, take the aspirin, you'll feel better."

Sitting up, she took the pills from his hand, popped them into her mouth and chased them with the coffee. "Thanks."

"No problem. I just saw that you were a little wobbly when you left last night, and thought you might have a big head this morning."

"Why are you being nice to me? What do you want?"

He laughed aloud. "Now is that anyway to talk to the man who just brought you medicine for your aching head?"

"Yes. At least until I find out what you want." She rubbed her temples.

"Not a thing, darlin'. Just trying to help." With that, he left her sitting there alone.

Marie McGaha

What was he up to now, being nice for no reason at all? Her head hurt too badly just then to figure it out. There was a knock on the door and Janet entered the room.

"Good morning," Janet said brightly. Waiting until Allison took a few more sips of her coffee, Janet continued, "You are wanted in Jason's office in about fifteen minutes. They'll be going over the new contract with you."

"Thanks, Janet." Allison attempted a smile, which, thankfully, didn't hurt too much. She walked down the hall to Jason's office. Captain, who was also just arriving, greeted her.

"Good morning, Allison," he said, as he wrapped an arm around her and squeezed.

"Good morning, Captain."

Jason's secretary escorted them to his office, shut the door softly, and left the room. Stephen had already arrived and sat with an ankle resting comfortably on his other knee. He grinned broadly, as Captain motioned for Allison to take the middle chair next to him, but Allison wouldn't give him the satisfaction of even glancing his way. Captain took a chair for himself and Jason handed out copies of the contract to everyone.

"I'll read the items listed in the contract for everyone's benefit, and if there are any points of contention, just let me know and we'll work them out. Any questions before we start?" Jason asked, smiling at Allison.

Marie McGaha

"No, not yet," Allison replied, trying to focus on the paper in her hand. Jason read through the contract and Allison had no objections to anything. They were being more than fair to her and if she had to object to anything, it would have been that they were being too generous.

~ * ~

Captain thought of what he'd just seen as he walked Allison back to her office. Glancing over at Stephen during the meeting, he'd observed a look in his son's eyes he'd never seen before, a look that was directed at Allison while she studied the contract. He guessed that his son had finally met the woman he would give his heart to, then he chuckled at the thought, and took a seat in front of Allison's desk.

She felt a little nervous. "Did you want to talk to me about something, Captain?"

"I just want to make sure you're comfortable here, Allison," he said with a fatherly smile.

"Oh yes, I love it here. It feels like home to me, Captain. I've never been happier."

"I'm glad to hear it. Now that you have the contract, you can think about finding a place of your own."

"Of course, I'm sorry. I should have thought about that. You'll want the room."

He shook his head. "Allison, I only brought it up because the room is so small, I thought you'd want a larger place. As far as I'm concerned, you

Marie McGaha

can live there for the rest of your life. I was just thinking that I know of a couple of places you might like."

"Oh, thank you, Captain. I would like that." She smiled affectionately at him.

"I don't suppose you've had the chance to call your mother?"

"No, not yet. I was going to call her last night, but it was too late, so I'll call her this evening. She's going to just freak."

"That's a good thing, I hope?" He raised a brow and smiled.

Allison laughed. "Yes, it's a good thing."

"Maybe you should invite her to come for a visit. You could show her around, let her do a little gambling. The family could get to know her."

Allison nodded, knowing he meant he wanted to get to know her family better, wanted to see what kind of family she came from. "I'd love to see her, it's been two years."

"That's far too long, Allison. Call her now and put the trip on your expense account," he said.

"That's a personal expense, Captain." Allison shook her head. "It's against the rules, and I'd never think of taking advantage of you like that."

Captain laughed heartily. "Darlin' you would hardly be taking advantage of me, but call Janet in here."

Marie McGaha

Allison picked up the phone and dialed the extension. "Janet, the Captain would like to see you, please."

A few seconds later, Janet opened the door. "Yes, Captain?"

"Allison is going to invite her mother for a visit and I want you to make the flight arrangements, and charge them to my personal account."

"Yes, sir," Janet said and shut the door.

"Captain, I can't let you do that. You pay me very well and I can afford to pay for the flight myself."

"I know, but I'm paying for it," he said with finality as he stood. "Call your mother and then give Janet the information so she can make the arrangements." He walked out of her office leaving her staring at the closed door.

Marie McGaha

~ Five ~

Allison waited anxiously at the airport for her mother's flight to land. It had been far too long since she'd seen her, and Allison was so excited she could hardly contain herself.

Captain had taken her to look at some homes for sale, and he'd found one just west of Gulfport that was perfect for her. With huge bay windows that peered out over a large veranda, Allison would be able to see the water whether she was sitting in the living room, or out on the porch swing. There were two bedrooms and each one had its own bathroom. The kitchen was large and airy, and there was a fenced back yard. Allison thought she might get a dog now. She'd always wanted one, but never had the space.

After she signed the papers with the realty company, she hugged Captain. She had never owned her own home before. Allison was so excited she couldn't wait until her mother arrived so she could show her the house. She had spent the last two weeks furnishing her new home, and by the time she had to meet her mother at the airport, Allison thought the house looked perfect.

Seeing her mother come into the terminal, she waved excitedly until she caught her attention. Trudy Hamstead's face lit up. Jumping up and down and throwing her arms around her mother's neck, Allison cried, "Oh, Mama, I'm so happy you're here."

ONE GOOD MAN

Marie McGaha

"Let me look at you." Her mother held Allison's face in both hands, as tears of joy shone in her eyes. "You are so beautiful and grown up. I can't believe it's been two years."

"Thank you, Mama, but I look like I always did."

Her mother shook her head. "No, you don't. You look happy and there's a sparkle in your eyes."

Allison hugged her mother. "I am happy here, Mama. I've missed you so much. Let's get your luggage and go home. I still can't believe I own my own home now."

"I'm so proud of you baby. I always knew you'd make it. You were always smarter than I ever was."

"Don't say that. If not for you, I wouldn't have gone to college or learned any of the things I did. You are the greatest mom in the world."

Trudy laughed and squeezed Allison's hand as they walked. "Thank you, sweetheart. So tell me all about your new job."

"I love working at the casino. Everyone is so friendly and they pay me way too much. Wait until you meet Captain. He's wonderful. Like having the father I always wanted. He can appear gruff sometimes, but he really isn't. I think he used to be a really handsome man before he got old."

"Allison!"

Marie McGaha

Allison laughed. "You know what I mean. He really is old enough to be my grandfather. But you'd never know from the way he gets around.

"Wait until you meet Shelly, she's like having a big sister, and she has three of the cutest kids you've ever seen. And they aren't brats either."

They retrieved Trudy's luggage and hauled the bags out to Allison's car, as she continued to talk about her job at the casino. Maneuvering her way out of the airport onto Hewes Avenue, Allison drove south until she reached Beach Boulevard and headed west a couple of miles to her driveway. She pulled the car under the carport, popped the trunk to pull out the suitcases, and then led the way through the back door. Allison led her mother through the kitchen and living room, then down the hall to the bedroom she'd set up for her. She set the luggage down and turned around.

"Do you like it?"

"It's perfect, baby," her mother said.

"I know how much you like peach and white, so I decorated just for you. I want you to stay here with me Mama."

"But I have a job in California that I have to get back to." She smoothed her daughter's hair.

"No you don't, Mama." Allison held her mother's hand. "You could stay with me. I make enough money to support both of us."

"I couldn't live off of you, Allison. I have to pay my own way."

Marie McGaha

"Then you could get a job here somewhere. There are lots of jobs to be had for those who want them. Please think about it, Mama."

"I will, Allison. But I'm not promising anything." She smiled.

"That's all I ask, and I know that once you're here for a few days, you'll love this place as much as I do."

"Okay, okay," Trudy said with a laugh.

"Now we have to get ready to go. Captain wants us to meet him for dinner at eight. Wear something pretty, Mama, I want everyone to see how beautiful you are."

"Allison, I didn't come all the way out here to flirt with your boss."

"I didn't say flirt with him, just you know—I want to show you off."

"Okay, I'll wear a mini skirt and go-go boots."

"You'll wear what? Oh, I get it. Ha-ha, Mama."

Her mother laughed. "What if I just put something on and you can tell me if you approve?"

"Okay. My room is just next door, if you need anything. I'm going to take a shower."

~ * ~

They drove to The Golden Lady, and Allison led her mother through the casino to the banquet room. Allison was almost as nervous as her mother, but couldn't wait to introduce her to the Collins family.

Marie McGaha

She thought her mother was the most beautiful woman in the world. When she'd seen her mother dressed in the white satin slacks, matching sleeveless jacket belted with a wide satin sash, she had grinned from ear to ear. Her mother had a wonderful figure, even for a woman of forty-three, and her breasts were still firm. Her hair was a little darker than Allison's, and she wore it longer, but it was easy enough to see the resemblance between mother and daughter. Trudy didn't look forty-three, and had been told on several occasions that she could pass for thirty-five. Allison led her mother into the banquet room and all eyes turned.

She grinned and said, "This is my mother, Trudy. Mama, this is, well, everyone."

Captain felt his heart leap as he stood and took Trudy's hand. "Welcome to Mississippi, Trudy."

"Mama this is Captain." Allison looked at him. "I've told her all about you." And desperately hoped they would like each other.

"I am so pleased to make your acquaintance. Allison has told me so much about you." Trudy looked over at the table, and said, "All of you. From what she's told me, I feel like I'm meeting celebrities."

"Trudy, the pleasure is all mine," Captain said as he shook Trudy's hand. "Please, sit down next to me."

Trudy smiled shyly. "Thank you."

Marie McGaha

While Captain and Trudy continued to talk, Stephen managed to maneuver Allison into the empty chair beside him and she frowned when he grinned. Clearing her throat, Allison spoke.

"Mama, this is Stephen." She jerked a thumb toward him. "Sitting next to him is Jason, Shelly, and their kids, Scotty, Jenny, and Davey. And this is Janet and her friend, Adam."

"Lovely to meet all of you," Trudy said as she looked at each person and smiled.

They all said hello, and Allison was so happy that the people who felt like family to her would have the chance to get to know her mother. Perhaps knowing them would help her mother make the decision to remain in Mississippi, Allison hoped.

Throughout dinner, Allison listened to the pleasant chatter, adding her voice when necessary, and avoiding eye contact with Stephen. Noticing her mother and Captain spent a lot of time in deep conversation, she was afraid he might be grilling Trudy about personal matters.

"What's the matter, Allison?" Stephen asked.

Glancing up at him, she asked, "What?"

"Are you all right? You're chewing your lip."

"It's nothing. I'm fine."

"No, it's something, or you wouldn't be looking like that." He chuckled. "Are you worried about your mother talking to my father?"

"I just hope he doesn't say something to frighten her, you know how he can be."

Marie McGaha

He laughed. "Yes, I do. But from where I'm sitting, I don't think you have anything to worry about."

"Really?"

"Really. I think my father finds your mother intriguing, Allison. You know he's been single a long time and that's not like him. Hey, we might wind up being related."

"What? Oh, no, I don't think... really?"

Stephen laughed. "You need to lighten up, darlin'. You're way too serious tonight. Here." He handed her the wine glass she hadn't touched. "Drink up." She did and he filled her glass again.

Allison was drinking too much she knew, and when Captain asked her mother if she'd like a tour of the boat she stood to go with them.

"Oh, that sounds like a good idea," Allison said.

"I think we'll be fine on our own, Allison. Don't you?" Trudy told her daughter. "You stay here and have fun with your friends."

"Sure, Mom," Allison said. She sat and downed another glass of wine. Allison spent time talking to Jason and Shelly until they excused themselves, saying they had to get the kids to bed. Not long after, Janet and her friend also left, and Allison found herself alone with Stephen.

"I have to find my mom," she told him and drained her glass.

"No you don't. She's perfectly safe, Allison."

Marie McGaha

"Yeah, but I'd feel better if I knew where they were," she said and looked at him.

"Okay, come on. I'll help you look for her. They didn't go far, I assure you."

He grabbed an unopened bottle of wine and held the door for her.

"I didn't see them inside, did you?" he asked innocently.

"No, but are you sure Captain would have brought her outside?"

He shrugged. "It's a nice night for a walk on the beach."

"Okay, but if we don't see them in a few minutes, we go back inside and look again."

"No problem," he said grinning. He pulled the loosened cork from the bottle, took a drink, then handed it to her and she tipped it up.

"Why don't you like me, Allison?" He drank from the bottle again.

"I like you just fine, Stephen." She took the bottle from his hand and tipped it up. She didn't hand it back.

"You don't act like it."

She took another long pull from the bottle and he reached for it. She ignored him, so he put his hands in his pockets and grinned to himself. He knew she was a lightweight when it came to drinking and figured she was well on her way to being snockered.

Marie McGaha

"It's not you I don't like. It's everything you are that I don't like." She tipped the bottle back again.

"Oh well, now I understand." He laughed. "What is it that I am that you don't like?"

"You know very well what you are, Stephlin, I mean Stephen," she corrected her mistake and took another drink.

"Why don't you tell me while I take a drink of that wine?" He didn't want her too drunk to know what she was doing when he kissed her. And he was going to kiss her.

"You're gorgeous, first of all." She pulled on the bottle again, ignoring his request for a drink. "And you're too smart, and too good looking. And women want you. And you're too gorgeous," she said as she hit the bottle again. This time he took it from her hand and she didn't even seem to notice. She staggered to the right and he grabbed her around the waist. "Let go of me."

"No problem, just trying to help."

"I don't need help from the licks of you, I mean the *likes* of you," she corrected herself again. "Men like you have a string of gorgeous women listed in your lil black blook, book, I mean. And men like you don't even look at women like me. And I hate all of you. You know, I might be fat, but I have a heart, and I feel things too, and I think you should all be ashamed."

"And you know this from experience?"

70

Marie McGaha

"Oh, yes I do." She wobbled, but caught herself. "Wesley Smothers."

"Who's that?"

"Who?"

"Wesley Smothers."

She stopped and poked a finger in his chest. "Who told you about Wesley? I don't ever want to hear that name again."

Chuckling, he said, "All right, I won't mention him again."

"Good, cause he's not worse mentioning." She didn't correct herself this time and neither did he.

"Why not?" Stephen prodded her. A little more walking and fresh air would do her good.

"Because he said he loved me and he moved in with me and he took my best friend. He was jus' usin' me. He din care 'bout me. He's a liar."

She spoke with such a mixture of anger and pain that he wanted to hold her, but kept his hands in his pockets. "He left you for another woman?"

"Yes," she said. "But doesn' matter. I'm here and he won't know where I am."

"You want him back?"

"Gawd noooooo," she shouted.

Stephen laughed. "Okay. So because of him you don't like me?"

"No, I don't like you cuz I like you too much and ish jus stupid of me."

"I don't think you're stupid, Allison. I think you're very pretty."

Marie McGaha

Allison burst into laughter then. "Pah-leese, you think I'm pretty? Yeah, right."

She started walking away from him before he could answer, and went toward the water, so he followed. She began taking off her shirt and said, "I want to swim. Less swim."

"Come on Allison, we can't go swimming tonight." He caught her hands and pulled her shirt back down.

She leaned into him. "Why not?"

"It's too late to go swimming," he told her.

"You're gorgeous," she whispered, looking into his eyes. He grinned and then she kissed him.

Surprised by her action, he kissed her back before he realized what he was doing. And he liked it, which also surprised him. Putting his arms around her, he could feel her body against his, and he didn't think that was bad at all. Then he slipped a hand beneath her top, but when he realized where they were, he stopped. Breaking the kiss, he looked at her. Her eyes were still closed.

Then she whispered, "Wesley."

He grasped her arms and pushed her away from him. "Allison. Stop." He shook her slightly and her eyes opened. "Allison." Her eyes went wide and she pushed at him. He fell over backwards in the sand.

"What are you doing?" She yelled.

He stood, glaring at her. "My name is Stephen, *not* Wesley. And the next time you kiss me, I'll

Marie McGaha

thank you to remember that." He grabbed her by the hand and half dragged her back to the casino.

~ * ~

There was an icky, fuzzy taste in her mouth when she woke the next morning, and her head was pounding. She looked around and saw she was in one of the casino hotel rooms. Her mother was in the other bed, sleeping peacefully. Allison had no memory of how she'd gotten into bed, but she did remember drinking too much and being on the beach kissing... *oh my goodness!*

She had been kissing Stephen and called him Wesley. She didn't know which was worse, the fact that she'd thrown herself at a man she claimed she didn't even like, or the fact that she *had* liked being that close to him? And she had no answer for why she had called him Wesley, because she had no desire to be kissing Wesley ever again. Well, crap, Stephen wouldn't let her live this one down.

Marie McGaha

~ Six ~

Allison was humiliated beyond belief and all because of Stephen. Pushing back the covers, she stumbled into the bathroom and took a shower—what she would have given for a toothbrush right then, so she called the front desk and had two sent to the room, along with some coffee and aspirin. Then she put her clothes back on and went to sit on the edge of the bed beside her mother.

Pushing back a lock of hair from her mother's forehead, Allison smiled. "Good morning, Mama."

Trudy smiled and patted her daughter's leg. "How are you feeling this morning? I thought you'd be asleep half the day with as much as you had to drink last night."

"Sorry about that. I didn't mean to drink so much, but after you left with Captain, oh ... I don't know, Stephen makes me crazy. Where did you two disappear to anyway? I was looking for you."

"He showed me around the casino, took me to the top deck and we looked at the lights and the ocean, and we talked half the night. I didn't even realize how late it had gotten until Stephen had us paged and told me that he'd put you to bed in here."

"Wait, wait, what? *Stephen* put me to bed?"

"He said you'd drunk just a little too much, and thought it best to put you to bed and then find me. Captain said there was no problem with us spending the whole weekend here if we wanted to."

"No, he wouldn't mind." Allison rubbed her head with both hands. She was wearing only a bra and panties when she woke up, so that meant Stephen had undressed her as well. She was embarrassed at the idea that Stephen had seen her practically naked. How she would ever face him again, she didn't know.

"We'll go back home as soon as you're ready, Mama," Allison said as she went to find her shoes.

"I, um, I have a date tonight, Allison," Trudy told her.

Allison stopped dead. "A date? You have a date? With who?" But she already knew the answer.

"Captain, who else?" Allison stared, mute. "I hope this is all right with you, baby. I really like him, and we had so much to talk about. He is the most intelligent, witty man I've met in years. And he's a handsome devil, too."

Allison shook her head. "He's old enough to be *your* father."

"Oh, don't be such a prude, Allison. Age doesn't matter. Your father and I were the same age and look how that turned out."

"That's not what I mean, Mother. I love Captain, but he's been married four times." Allison sat down and slipped her shoes on.

"I know, he told me. But it's a date, Allison, not a marriage proposal."

Marie McGaha

"I know. I guess I just didn't expect you to like him in that way."

Trudy laughed. "Sweetie, I haven't liked anyone in *that* way in so long, I'm not sure I even remember what *that* is."

Allison answered the knock on the door and brought the toothbrushes and coffee into the room. Her hangover wasn't as bad as she first thought, but the aspirin she washed down with coffee still did wonders. When both women were ready, Allison led Trudy down the hall and outside to her car. They made the drive back to Allison's house, and as Allison changed her clothes, the phone rang.

"Hello?"

"Hi, darlin', can I speak to your gorgeous mother?"

Allison rolled her eyes. "Of course, Captain, just a moment. Mom, phone." When her mother picked up, Allison hung up the extension.

"Sweetie," Trudy said a few minutes later as she walked into Allison's room. "Captain has invited us to go sailing on the gulf today. I told him yes, so I hope you want to go, too."

Allison almost said no, but then thought, if her mother was going to be on the ocean with Captain, she wasn't letting her go alone. "Of course." She smiled brightly. "Do you have a bathing suit with you?"

"I brought one just in case. He wants us to meet him at the casino in half an hour."

Marie McGaha

"Then we better get going." Allison grabbed her own one-piece suit, shoved it into her beach bag with some tanning lotion and tossed it over her shoulder.

~ * ~

Allison didn't know much about boats, but she knew what she liked and she really liked Captain's boat, *The Painted Lady*. With a fully stocked galley, two full baths, sleeping quarters for ten, a swimming pool and Jacuzzi on deck, Allison couldn't figure out why he didn't live on board. She knew, if the beautiful boat belonged to her, that's exactly where she'd live.

After showing them around, Captain led them back on deck in time to greet Jason and Shelly who arrived without their kids, and their nanny. Just as they were getting ready to get underway, Stephen showed up. Allison ignored him when he grinned at her. She would just make sure that she stayed as far from him as possible.

He didn't make it possible.

Laying a towel on the chaise lounge, she got comfortable with a glass of iced tea; there would be no alcohol for Allison today. As Stephen slid a chair alongside hers, settling in as if invited, Allison decided the only thing to do was ignore him.

"Not speaking to me today, huh?" He laughed. "Well, that's understandable." He waited, knowing the remark would get a rise from her.

Marie McGaha

"What do you mean it's *understandable*?" she asked tersely.

"Well, after the way you threw yourself at me last night, I can understand why you'd be too embarrassed to speak to me today."

"I did not throw myself at you."

"Sure."

"I didn't."

"Okay, we did kind of throw ourselves at each other," he admitted.

"I was tipsy and didn't know what I was doing. It will not happen again, believe me."

"So you have to be tipsy to kiss me?"

"Yes. No. Oh, shut up."

He laughed and took a drink of her iced tea. "But you do kiss pretty good."

"Remember it because you'll never get another one."

"And you looked good in your bra and panties, too."

She inhaled sharply and sat up straight.

"You, you... you *pig*. You could have just left my clothes alone. You could have put me on the bed without undressing me. And just what else did you do?"

"What are you talking about?"

"You know exactly what I'm talking about. What else did you do while you were undressing me?"

Marie McGaha

"Do you think so little of me to believe that I would take advantage of a woman who's passed out?"

"Oh, I really do think little of you, believe that."

"I don't take advantage of women, Allison," he said in a calm voice that belied the emotion flashing in his dark eyes. "I don't have to take advantage of a woman who is passed out. And if you want the truth, you wouldn't have objected one bit when you were wrapped around me out there on the beach."

"Only because I thought you were Wesley." The words rolled off her tongue, although she didn't know why she lied. Something flashed across his face, and disappeared just as quickly. But when he leaned into her, the look in his eyes almost caused her to flinch.

His voice barely above a whisper, he vowed, "Believe this Allison, when I do have you, and know that I will, my name will be the only one you speak with that beautiful mouth." He let the tip of one finger slide sensuously over her bottom lip, then stood and left her alone.

Watching as he disappeared down the galley steps, Allison's heart continued to beat radically for a full five minutes. She thought he was going to kiss her right there, but he didn't. How could she possibly feel disappointed that he hadn't?

Marie McGaha

"I don't know what game you're playing, but you're playing with the wrong girl," Allison muttered under her breath, and lifted the cold glass of tea to her forehead.

Looking around to make sure no one else had seen what happened, she concluded that the two couples seemed too engrossed in one another to notice. Allison felt nauseous. Her gaze landed on her mother and Captain and she shook her head. A nuclear bomb could detonate next to the boat and neither of them would be aware. Glancing over to Jason and Shelley, she found they were just as involved in a conversation and oblivious to anyone around them. Allison shook her head again.

"Sheesh, is this a conspiracy to see how miserable they can make me?" She said to herself.

"Did you say something, baby?" Trudy asked.

"No, Mama," Allison said with a shake of her head.

She wanted a boyfriend, she really did, but there just weren't any men around that suited her. Well, there was Stephen, but he was hardly boyfriend material, and just as soon as she was desperate enough for a one-night stand, she'd call him first. Until then, she was apparently doomed to watch her mother making out with her boss. *Eeew!* She got up and went down to the galley to find a snack.

~ * ~

Marie McGaha

"The weather is just lovely, Captain," Trudy said.

"It's like this almost year round. And please, call me Nelson," he replied. "I hear southern California is the same way."

"Not really, Nelson. It is warm year round, but nothing like this. In California, the air is stale, sometimes brown and sometimes orange, depending on the smog level. And it smells pretty bad most of the time." She laughed. "I can see why Allison fell in love with this place."

"Speaking of Allison, you know I've grown quite fond of your daughter," he said. "She's been a real asset to the company for the three months she's been with us. I expect by the time she's been here a year, we won't be able to get along without her."

"I'm so glad. She's been my life, and it means so much to me to know that she's really found a place to belong."

"How about you, Trudy? Have you found a place to belong?"

Looking at him for a moment, she licked her lips. "I don't know. I've always lived in California, and never really gave it much thought. But Allison wants me to stay with her and to move out here permanently."

"Are you considering it?"

"I don't know."

ONE GOOD MAN

Marie McGaha

Taking her hand in his, he lifted it to his mouth. "Consider it, Trudy," he said in a smoky voice that sent goose bumps over her body.

Trudy remembered the feeling—vaguely. It had been twenty-five years since she'd first met Allison's father at eighteen, just having graduated high school. Five years older, he seemed so worldly and well-traveled. He claimed to have hitchhiked around Europe, something Trudy wanted to do, but just never seemed to be able to afford the plane ticket. He promised to take her places, show her things she'd only dreamed of, and even though her grandparents who'd raised her objected, she married him.

Nothing turned out exactly as he promised, and by the time she discovered she was pregnant, they were fighting all the time. There was no money for food if they paid the rent, no money for rent if they bought food and paid the electric bill, so when she announced she was pregnant, John Hamstead flipped out. When Trudy was nearly six months pregnant, John told her he had an offer in Modesto for a better paying job. He never came back.

Since then, she spent most of her life working two jobs to support her daughter, and didn't have the time, or the energy, to date. When Allison was in high school, a co-worker asked Trudy out and she'd accepted. She found out quickly how dating had changed, and when she refused to sleep with him, he called her an unkind name and left her to find her own way home. A short time after Allison

Marie McGaha

moved to Chicago, Trudy attempted dating one more time and went out with a friend of her next-door neighbor's. After three dates, the relationship became intimate, and then he and his ex-wife decided to patch things up.

Trudy figured she would never meet another man she would like to date, much less find one she would consider having a relationship with, until she met Captain. He made her feel things she hadn't felt in far too long, and as much as that frightened her, she also felt excited. He was warm, easy to talk to, funny, charming, and so intelligent. She felt as if they'd known one another forever, and she found herself looking at him, wondering what it would be like to kiss him.

He caught her looking at him with her bottom lip caught in her teeth as she studied him.

"Why are you looking at me like that?" He grinned when she blushed.

"No reason," she said with a smile.

~ * ~

Allison found the galley well-stocked and pulled a basket of strawberries from the refrigerator along with a tub of dipping chocolate and a can of whipped cream. Checking around the corner to make sure she could indulge in a little decadence without anyone catching her, she took the treats to the booth-style table and slid around to the backside where she wouldn't be seen immediately if someone came below deck. She took one large berry by its

Marie McGaha

stem, dipped it in the chocolate, and sucked it into her mouth. Then, she held the whipped cream can upside down and squirted. Her eyes rolled up in the back of her head as she chewed. This was heaven.

Finishing the first berry, she picked up a second and repeated the process. As she dipped the fruit, she looked at the can of whipped cream and shrugged, then tipped her head back and filled her mouth with the white cream. She followed that with a berry dripping chocolate. On the fourth one, she waited until she'd eaten the whole thing before filling her mouth with whipped cream. When she righted her head, she almost choked. Stephen stood casually leaning against the wall, grinning from ear to ear.

"I heard the most peculiar sound," he said.

"What?" She asked as she swallowed.

He pointed. "The noise from a whipped cream can."

Frowning at him, she noticed there was chocolate all over her hands and licked them clean. Seeing the amused look on Stephen's face, she stuck her tongue out at him, causing laughter to pour from his lips. Pushing out from behind the table, she went to the sink and washed.

"I could help you get that chocolate off your fingers," he offered.

"What is your problem, Stephen? Why don't you just go back to seducing Ms. April, or whatever

Marie McGaha

other woman you have on your short little string, and leave me alone?"

"Why do you try to make me angry, Allison? What have I done to cause you to treat me so badly?"

"I don't treat you any way at all," she said.

"You treat me with contempt."

"Look Stephen, sometimes two people just rub each other the wrong way, and that's all there is to it. Can't we just leave it at that?"

"Sure we could, except that's not what you told me last night," he said as a wicked grin spread across his face.

When would she figure out that no matter what he said, he was just baiting her?

"I was drunk last night," she said.

"But not so drunk you don't remember kissing me and wrapping yourself around me the way you did."

"Again, I thought you were Wesley." She glared at him.

He stood and looked at her coolly for a moment before he turned and walked out. She grinned. She'd found how to get him in a way he couldn't fight against. Putting the berries and other items back in the fridge, she went back on deck.

~ Seven ~

It was after eight that evening by the time the boat docked, and Stephen had not spoken to her since the encounter in the galley, which suited Allison just fine. She was sunburned, tired, and ready to go home and fall into bed. Her mother had a date with Captain and told her not to wait up. She rolled her eyes and her mother laughed. Captain came to the house to pick up Trudy after giving her time to shower and change. He kissed Allison on the cheek.

"You have my cell number. You can call anytime if you get worried about your mother. But I promise to take good care of her."

"Great," Allison mumbled and shut the door behind them. Climbing into bed, she fell asleep in a matter of minutes.

~ * ~

Nelson knew how to impress a woman. Two-dozen red roses waited in the car for Trudy as he opened the door for her. She smiled and held them to her face, inhaling the fragrance. He told the driver to take them to the airport, where a chartered flight to Denver awaited them, followed by a limo waiting to take them to Vale. It was April, but in the Rockies, there was still snow on the ground and the feel of winter in the air. As they checked into Deer Lodge Ski Resort, and made their way to the private condominium, Trudy's heart beat so fast she thought she might have a heart attack.

Marie McGaha

"I didn't bring anything with me," she told Nelson. "I don't have a jacket or a change of clothes."

"Don't worry about that. I've taken care of everything." He squeezed her shoulder affectionately. And indeed he had taken care of everything. When he opened the door to their suite, she found he bought everything she would need, including an elegant evening gown, a beautiful dress, two changes of casual clothing, a complete ski outfit and a full-length fur coat.

"Oh my... I can't believe you did this. I appreciate it, but there's no way I can accept this," Trudy gasped.

"Why not?"

"Because... I just can't. We've barely just met and I wouldn't feel right accepting these things from you."

"Fine, then just borrow them," he said casually.

"How can I borrow them?"

"You just wear the ones you want and when we leave, just leave them on the bed."

"I don't know," she said slowly, fingering the fur coat and then the beautiful gown. "Could I really?"

"Why not? Borrowing a few things won't hurt anyone. We'll be leaving tomorrow evening, so what's the difference?"

Marie McGaha

"All right," Trudy agreed. "If I can just borrow them."

"Good, now pick out something to wear to dinner. I think the blue dress will look beautiful on you," he suggested.

"Okay." She caught her bottom lip in her teeth as she picked up the dress and the matching shoes, and went into the bedroom to change. Standing in front of the mirror, she twirled around. She felt that she looked beautiful and wished she could dress in such lovely clothing all the time, but it was nice to be able to borrow this one if only for an evening. When she came into the living room, Nelson gave a low whistle.

"I was right, blue definitely looks beautiful on you."

"Thank you." She smiled shyly.

"It's cold out, you better wear this." As he held the fur coat for her, she almost purred as she slid her arms into the sleeves. He crooked his arm and she accepted. They went down the elevator and waited as the driver opened the limo door for them.

The restaurant sat high on a mountaintop, the entire front of the building was of paned glass overlooking the lights of the town below, making a breathtaking view.

"Thank you for this lovely evening, Nelson," Trudy said over drinks.

"You're welcome." He smiled as he reached across the table and took her hand.

Marie McGaha

"I haven't been out like this in so long, I barely remember," she said with a chuckle.

"You should be wined and dined on a regular basis."

"You're too kind."

"I'm just honest."

"No, I mean with everything you've done for Allison and me. You've gone way beyond the call of duty."

"I didn't give Allison anything she didn't earn. You raised a good girl."

Trudy smiled. "I did, didn't I?"

Nelson raised his glass. "To you. A wonderful mother and a beautiful woman."

Although she smiled, Trudy felt her cheeks grow warm and knew she was blushing. "Thank you. Now, what about you, Nelson? I get the feeling you earned everything you have."

Nodding, he replied, "Yes, I did. I was born in Ireland to a family who immigrated to New York City when I was just a year old. We lived in Hell's Kitchen, a really rough neighborhood that required more brawn than brains to survive. Most of my friends wound up either dead or in prison, and I just couldn't see that as my fate.

"I hitchhiked across the country, worked odd jobs, whatever I could find that paid enough to keep me from starving to death. One day I wound up in Las Vegas and landed a job cleaning up one of the casinos. That was really my lucky break."

Marie McGaha

"Lucky? How?"

"After about six months, I became friends with one of the pit bosses and he taught me the ropes and helped me get a job in the pit. I learned as much as I could about gambling and running a casino, and used my pay to take business and finance classes at the college. I worked twelve and fourteen hour days, so I didn't have a lot of time for school, and it took me a year longer than everyone else to get my degree, but I graduated."

Trudy smiled affectionately. "Oh, Nelson, you are such a special man."

"Don't give me a big head now," he chuckled, as he continued his story.

"A few months later, a little casino in Border Town offered me a job. Back then, Border Town was barely a town. It was more like one last chance to lose a little money on your way home. But the position as pit boss allowed me to put away enough money to buy my own place. And when the boys came along, I put them to work as soon as they were old enough. They swept floors, emptied ashtrays, and scrubbed toilets. I also told them, if they wanted to work with me, they had to go to college first. Of course, by then I had the money and they both have degrees in business.

"When the state of Mississippi allowed floating casinos, I bought one and moved south. I've never regretted any of it."

Marie McGaha

"You should be so proud of yourself, and of your sons. You're a remarkable man."

"Thank you, but enough about me," he said, as a waiter brought their food. "Thank you, son, just in time."

When they finished eating and had gone back to the lodge, Trudy was happy she'd come. The mountain air was fresh and fragrant, having been cleaned by many snowfalls since last summer. Since the summer tourist season hadn't yet begun, there weren't many people about.

Nelson helped Trudy out of the fur and tossed it onto the sofa. Wrapping an arm around her waist, he pulled her to him. His lips pressed hers gently, tasting her, letting her get used to him. She didn't stop him, but he could feel her nervousness. Knowing she hadn't had much experience with men, and her most recent experience had been three dates two years ago, Nelson was prepared to take this at whatever pace she wanted.

"Trudy, there are two bedrooms here," he said looking into her eyes. "I'm in no hurry, and if you want to wait, it's no problem at all."

Looking into the dark depths of his eyes, seeing the concern, and the caring there, she shook her head slightly. Lowering his mouth to hers again, he gently and slowly touched her lips. He nipped her bottom lip with his teeth. Her mouth opened to him and he felt her body give in to his. The kiss deep-

Marie McGaha

ened and Nelson suddenly felt himself caught up in a fury of need.

~ * ~

Nelson Collins had been married four times, each one a brief event. Married for only four months to his first wife, Candy, who was a young stripper he'd met in Las Vegas, he didn't think that one should even really count. He'd married Grace a year later, and she'd given him both of his sons. She was a pretty, young thing and he was forty years old by then, but he was happy with Grace, happy with his family, but five years later, she'd been killed in a car accident. Both of his sons had been in the car with her, and only a miracle had saved them from the same fate. He grieved her death, but with two young sons to raise and a business to run, he'd married Vanessa instead of hiring a nanny. In retrospect, he knew the nanny would have proven much cheaper in the long run than being married to Vanessa. When they finally divorced two years later, she tried to take half the casino with her.

His last wife had been a wonderful woman who loved his sons and they loved her, but he'd married Amelia for them and not for himself. He liked her just fine, and she was good to him, and treated his sons as if they were her own, but in the end, she also wanted a husband. When she didn't get one, she left him. She didn't hurt the boys, however, by abandoning them, and in fact, continued to see them every weekend, never missing a birthday, or

Marie McGaha

holiday with them. She attended the boys' gradua-
tions, was there when Jason married Shelly, and she
considered Jason's children her own grandchildren.
Even now, Nelson and Amelia were on friendly
terms. When she remarried, she invited Captain and
the boys to the wedding.

Since Amelia had left him, he'd not really had
the desire to date, and with *The Golden Lady* to take
care of, well, she was all the woman he could handle. Then Allison had come to work for him, and
he'd fallen in love with her in a very fatherly fash-
ion. When he suggested she bring her mother out for
a visit, it was simply because he saw the sadness in
her eyes when Allison spoke of her mother. He could
tell how much she missed her mother, and he wanted to do something to make her happy. But then
he'd met Trudy Hamstead, and he felt like a young
colt again.

Even though Trudy was young enough to be his
daughter, there was nothing fatherly in the way he
thought of her. Being nearly seventy had taught him
a few things in life, and the most important one was
that no one lived forever, and if you didn't grab
what you could, you'd wake up dead one day and
regret everything you never did. So he made the decision he was going to win Trudy's heart and marry
her.

Waking first the next morning, Trudy stretched, rolled toward him, and smiled as she watched

Marie McGaha

him sleeping. She felt like a brand new woman, and her body was gloriously stiff and sore. Sliding out of bed, she slipped his shirt on, though it was three sizes too big and hung to her knees. She rolled up the sleeves and padded into the bathroom first, then to the kitchen. When she opened the cupboards, she found a can of coffee and brewed a pot for them. There were a few groceries in the fridge as well, so she fixed a large omelet with mushrooms, onions and tomatoes, she made toast, fixed a tray, and added two cups filled with coffee. Holding a cup of coffee near Nelson's face, she laughed when he wrinkled his nose, still not wanting to wake up, so she kissed him. He opened his eyes and smiled.

"What are you doing up so early?"

She laughed. "It's nearly noon. And I fixed breakfast."

"Noon?" He scooted to a sitting position and took the coffee she offered. He couldn't remember the last time he'd slept until noon.

"Since I didn't know how you took your coffee, you got it black like mine. There is an omelet and toast on the tray as well. I don't know about you, but I'm starved." She settled onto the bed next to him and picked up a fork.

He watched her dig into the omelet and grinned as he took a drink of coffee. "I had a good time last night," he said.

"Me too," she said through a bite. "You were wonderful." She leaned over and kissed him.

Marie McGaha

He chuckled. "Thank you. But I was inspired by a very beautiful lady." He saw her blush. "Trudy," he said, taking her hand before she could fork up another bite. "I want to talk to you."

Setting the fork down, she swallowed a sip of the coffee, and hoped this wasn't the "it's been fun, have a great trip back to California" speech. *You shouldn't have read more into it than what was there.* When was she going to learn that men weren't looking for the fairy tale? Well, she should have known better, she was a grown woman for Pete's sake and just because they'd spent some time together, didn't mean they'd have any kind of relationship. Besides, men like Nelson didn't take up with women like her. He was a rich man, and rich men walked around with tall, leggy blondes on their arms.

"I want you to know that last night was the best of my life. You made an old man feel like a young man again. This trip did me more good than you'll ever know."

He paused and she braced herself.

"I hope that I was able to give you half the pleasure you gave me, Trudy. And I hope that you will know that what I'm about to say comes from my heart. I'm not a young man anymore, and this isn't exactly how I planned on doing this, but I'm afraid to give you time to think about it. What a beautiful woman like you would want with an old goat like me, I don't know, but I want you to marry me."

95

Marie McGaha

She opened her mouth ready to tell him she understood, she didn't expect anything from him, and he shouldn't feel responsible because it was her decision too. Her mouth opened, she shook her head in disbelief as what he said struck home.

"What?"

"I know this is sudden, but at my age, how much time do I have to waste?" He grinned a little then. "I fell in love with you when you walked into the banquet hall with Allison. And I would be so proud to have you as my wife."

Trudy shut her mouth, opened it only to shut it again. Her mind refused to accept what he had just said, or maybe her mind had just shut down and she no longer understood English the same way she had before.

"Trudy," the Captain said, "are you all right, darlin'?"

"I don't know," she said as she exhaled the breath she'd been holding. "Did you just ask me to *marry* you?"

He grinned. "Yes, I did. But darlin' you don't have to answer right now if you need time to think about it. I'll understand if you need more time to figure out how you feel about me. This isn't a limited time offer, you can take all the time you need."

"*You* want to marry *me*?" She breathed out again.

"Yes, I do. I should've given you a ring, but I wasn't going to ask until we got back home. I had

Marie McGaha

this whole romantic evening planned where I'd pro-
pose on one knee and give you the ring at the same
time, but after last night, I didn't want to give you
the chance to figure out that you can do better than
an old man like me."

"No, I can't," she said, shaking her head.

"You can't marry me?"

"No. Oh no, I can marry you, but I can't do
better than an old man like you," she said, disbelief
coating her voice.

He laughed and set his coffee down. "So you
will marry me?"

"I can't believe this, but yes, I will marry you,
Nelson."

"Because you love me?"

She shook her head. "No, I'll marry you because you're the best date I've ever had."

He threw his head back and laughed aloud.
"That's good enough for me."

She leaned in and kissed him. "Yes, Nelson,
I'll marry you because I love you."

Cupping the back of her head, he grasped her
shoulder with the other hand and rolled her over his
legs onto the bed, and kissed her.

Marie McGaha

~ Eight ~

Allison awoke the next morning feeling very sore from the sunburn she'd gotten on the boat the day before. She didn't usually burn, but she hadn't been tanning as much as she'd have liked to. And she was out in the sun all day thanks to Stephen who, although he ignored her, seemed to be every-where she wanted to be. She took a shower, then retrieved the Ocean Potion from the fridge and smoothed it over all of her tender, burnt skin.

Her mother hadn't called, and Allison consid-ered calling Captain's cell just to make sure every-thing was all right, but hey, her mother was a, well, she was *her mother*. How dare she stay out all night with a man she barely knew?

"Get a grip, Allison," she said and made a pot of coffee. If her mother wanted to stay out, who was she to complain? But didn't it just seem a little, well, *icky*? Especially since Allison wasn't seeing any-one herself, and hadn't since Wesley had started seeing Sarah. Every time she had tried to be roman-tic with him, he said he was too tired. *Yeah, too tired because he'd wasted all his energy on Sarah. Oh, get over it, Allison*, she admonished herself. She had a new life now, one that she loved.

With coffee in hand, she went into the bed-room and put on a pair of baggy shorts and a loose t-shirt with no bra, trying to keep her clothes from touching her sunburn. After making her bed, she

Marie McGaha

went into the bathroom to gather up the towels and put them in the laundry, when there was a knock on the door.

Stephen Collins stood on the veranda when she opened the door. Well, he wasn't really standing, no, he was *lounging* there like he owned the place. Without a word, she glared at him. And he smiled. *Oh for Pete's sake!*

"Aren't you going to invite me in?" He asked as he ran his eyes up and down her like he was standing in the ice cream aisle looking at all the delicious flavors he could choose from. Then he licked his lips. Rolling her eyes, Allison took a step back and allowed him entrance. Then shut the door a little harder than necessary.

"I smell coffee, mind if I have a cup?" With a wave of her arm, she pointed him in the direction of the kitchen. He was still smiling.

Allison went back to gathering up the laundry and headed to the washing machine. Stephen leaned against the doorjamb and watched her as she poured the soap and fabric softener into the little compartments. She shut the lid and turned the knob. Slid passed him without saying a word, and poured another cup of coffee, before sitting at the kitchen table to read the newspaper. *I can keep this up all day, buster, I'm on my own turf now,* she thought smugly.

Unfortunately, Stephen didn't appear at all perturbed by her rudeness. Without a word, he pour-

Marie McGaha

ed himself a cup of coffee, sat down at the table and took the newspaper out of her hand, divided it between them, giving her back the section she'd been reading. Biting her tongue, she knew he was baiting her. After a few minutes, she sneaked a peak around her share of the paper and saw that he was leaning comfortably back in the chair with one ankle propped up on his knee. *Oh, how I'd like to kick that chair right now!*

This little stalemate went on for half an hour until Allison finished her section of the paper and laid it on the table. Going to the counter, she brought the coffee pot back and filled her cup. Stephen held his out toward her, never taking his eyes off the paper. She blew an audible breath that made her hair puff out, but she filled his cup. As she set the pot on a trivet, he folded his part of the paper, passed it to her and picked up the part she'd been reading. Pulling her chair out noisily, she sat down, picked up the paper, and began reading again. Well, she wasn't actually reading, because she was seething instead. How arrogant could one man be? And she refused to give him the satisfaction of knowing he could get to her. Because he couldn't—get to her that is.

Finishing her coffee, she laid the paper down, while he continued to read and drink his coffee. All right, she'd had enough of this. "What are you doing here?" She finally asked him.

Marie McGaha

"Just waiting for you to speak to me," he said and laid the paper down.

"Okay, I'm talking to you. What do you want?"

"I came by to apologize for yesterday," he said gently.

That threw her. "What do you want to apologize for?" She asked, eyeing him warily.

"I want to apologize for whatever it was I did to make you angry with me. It seems that no matter what I say to you, I upset you. If I agree with you, you're mad, and if I disagree with you, you get mad. So, I apologize for whatever it is about me that seems to keep you angry all the time."

She stared at him. This was a new tactic, even if what he was saying were true. He did seem to set her off whenever he was around. And none of it was his fault. She was angry at him for something someone else had done to her, and that wasn't right. And being rude to him since the first time they met, even when he tried to be nice, was a reflex.

"Well," she said, unable to meet his gaze, "it's not your fault really. I should be apologizing to you for being rude when you really have just tried to be nice to me."

"That's all I wanted to hear," he said, getting up from the table.

"What? You arrogant... *That* is why I don't like you."

He laughed. "Calm down. I was just joking. You are really too serious. Try having a little fun

Marie McGaha

sometime instead of always looking for reasons to be angry at someone."

"You are the only one I'm angry with." She tried to hide the smile playing on her lips.

"See, smiling isn't so bad." He put a finger under her chin and tipped her face up a little. "I know you've got one in there somewhere."

"Stop it." She slapped his hand away, but smiled anyway.

Stephen felt his heart leap when he saw the sweet curve that brought out her dimples. He took a deep breath and forced himself back in his chair. "What are you doing today?"

"I was going to take my mom to New Orleans, but she apparently had a better offer."

Stephen chuckled. "So I heard. How about if I take you to New Orleans instead?"

"Really? You want to spend the day with me?"

"I do." He grinned. *More than you will ever know*, he added silently.

~ * ~

The drive to New Orleans was pleasant and Allison found there was a lot more to Stephen Collins than met the eye. When he wasn't trying to pick up a woman, or wasn't busy being arrogant, he was charming, witty and intelligent. She found out he had a degree in finance and business, just like she did, and he never wanted to do anything besides follow in his father's footsteps. He told her how his

Marie McGaha

mother and father had met when his father was already forty years old, so Stephen hadn't come along until his father was nearly forty-two. When he told her how his mother had died in an accident when he was four years old, and how his step-mother, Amelia, had continued to be part of his and Jason's lives even after she and his father divorced, Allison felt something near her heart break just a little. She hadn't realized until then how much they had in common.

Finally, Allison told him the whole story about Wesley and how he had cheated on her with her friend, Sarah. "But I'm over him now. I'm over both of them," she added.

Stephen smiled. "Are you sure?"

"Of course I'm sure. If not for Wesley being such a loser, I wouldn't be living here now. I love everything about the Gulf Coast. I love the casino, and I especially love your father. You and Jason are so lucky to have him."

"Most of the time, we're lucky to have him," Stephen said with a laugh. "You haven't seen him lose his temper yet. What about your father?"

"I don't know him. He ran out on us before I was born, and never came back. I had my grandfather of course, but he wasn't the same as having a father."

"I don't mind sharing mine with you, Allison," Stephen said softly, as he lifted her hand to his lips.

Marie McGaha

Allison felt another crack very near her heart, and swallowed hard. "How much farther is it?" She asked and withdrew her hand slowly.

"A few miles."

After he parked the car in a day lot, Stephen hired a carriage to take them on a tour of the French Quarter along Bourbon Street. They stopped at a street corner pub, where he bought Allison a peach daiquiri while he drank beer. When they finished their drinks, they walked up and down the streets and peeked into shops, watched the peculiar sights on the streets, and when he took her hand, she didn't pull away.

They rode the trolley to the Garden District and ate dinner on a riverboat on the Mississippi river. Allison was happy and tired when they finally went back to Stephen's car late that night. She tried to stay awake, but drifted off with her head on his shoulder and found herself shaken awake when he pulled into her driveway. Walking her to the door, he waited with his hands in his pockets as she put the key in the lock.

Turning to him, Allison said, "Thank you for today, Stephen. I had a really nice time."

"You're welcome," he said and kissed her cheek. He grinned and walked back to his Mustang.

Peeking into her mother's room, Allison found it empty. Checking the answering machine, Allison listened as her mother apologized for having reached

Marie McGaha

the machine instead of her daughter. "I'm really sorry, baby, but we flew to Colorado for dinner and then a storm blew in unexpectedly and we're snowbound for a while. We expect to get out of here in the morning. I love you. Kisses."

Allison pushed the delete button. "You don't sound too upset, Mother," she said to the machine.

Then she went to bed.

~ * ~

"Mmm," Allison moaned. "Oh, Stephen."

Her body vibrated as Allison bolted upright in bed. "Oh my," she said. "Why do I keep dreaming about him like that?" She looked at the clock on the nightstand. "I could've slept another hour."

Tossing back the blankets, she jumped out of bed and took a shower, dressed, cleaned house, folded her laundry, and made it to work by seven, which was still an hour early. At her desk, she booted her computer and went over what she'd done on Friday, then began working on the week to come. Grabbing the phone, she called Lynette, ordered a latte and a cinnamon bagel with hazelnut cream cheese and went back to work. A few minutes later, she heard the door open and didn't bother looking up.

"Just set it on the desk," she said without turning around.

"I think I'll just set it on a chair instead," Stephen said, grinning.

Marie McGaha

Allison spun her chair around. "Oh, I thought you were Lynette bringing my coffee and bagel. What are you doing here?"

"It's eight-thirty, I try to make it look as if I work here," he said blandly.

Allison smiled. "I didn't realize I'd been here that long." Lynette came in with the coffee and bagel just then. "Thank you so much. You're a life saver," she told the head of kitchen services.

"No problem. What about you Stephen, can I bring you anything?"

"No, I'll just share Allison's." He grinned and took half the bagel. Lynette shook her head and left.

"So, would you like some of my bagel?" Allison asked sardonically as he took a bite.

"Thanks, but I've got my own." He spread cream cheese over the bread. Allison smiled and picked up the other half of the bagel and took a bite. She took a drink of the latte and then passed it to Stephen. He took a drink, made a face, and gave it back to her.

"You don't drink lattes?" She asked as she took another drink.

"No sugar," he said licking cream cheese off his thumb.

"I don't like sugar in mine," she said with a smile. He was smiling too, really smiling. "What?"

"I like looking at you," he said.

Feeling her cheeks heat, she looked away and mumbled, "Um, I have to get back to work."

Marie McGaha

"What's wrong with me liking the way you look?"

She busied herself with some papers that apparently were in desperate need of rearranging. "I don't know."

"Then why did it embarrass you?"

"Mmm, it didn't," she said, but refused to look at him.

"Allison, look at me," he said softly. "Look at me." She raised her eyes and peered at him from under long lashes. He smiled. "I think you're beautiful and you may as well get used to me looking at you, 'cause I'm not going to stop."

Nodding, she said, "I really have a lot of work to do, Stephen."

"I'm leaving, but I'll be back around one to take you to lunch, all right?" She nodded as he left her office.

Downing the rest of her coffee, and turning back to the computer, she began working again. As she looked at the page on the screen, it flashed off for just a second and then came back on. "Hmm, that was weird," she said aloud. Then put it out of her mind as she continued to work.

Allison looked up when she heard a knock on the door. Janet popped her head in and said, "I'm here. Sorry to be so late."

"Don't worry about it. I actually didn't know you weren't here."

"Got in early, huh?"

Marie McGaha

"Yeah, I couldn't sleep."

"Well, if you need anything, I'm here."

"Thanks," Allison said, already distracted by her work once again.

She worked on the numbers for a while longer, but something just wasn't coming out right no matter what she entered. Rechecking the figures on the screen in front of her, she went backwards on the computer pages, and no matter how she read it, something was definitely wrong. Finally, unable to figure it out, she picked up the phone and dialed Janet's extension.

"Yes, Allison?"

"Can you come in here for a minute, Janet?"

Janet appeared a few seconds later. "What's up?"

"There's something weird going on and I can't figure it out."

"What do you mean?"

"I don't know exactly. I was going over what I'd done Friday and the computer blinked off, but came back on in just a second. When I started going over the work again, the figures were wrong, so I went back a week and no matter what I do, something isn't right."

"Let me take a look." Janet took Allison's chair, went back and forth over the pages and agreed with Allison. "I'll bet it's nothing more than a glitch in the system. I'll mention it to Captain."

Marie McGaha

"He's not back yet." Allison told her as she sat back down.

"Captain isn't here?" Janet said with surprise in her voice. "Where is he?"

"Oh, he and my mother went to Colorado and got snowed in," Allison said automatically, more concerned with what happened to her work.

"You're kidding?"

"What?" Allison looked up.

"Your mother and Captain? He hasn't even dated in like, forever. This is huge."

Allison stared at Janet. "You're making way too much of it. They just went on a little trip and got snowed in, that's all."

"If you say so, but Captain dating again? We just joked about him marrying number five because it's been so long since he even looked at a woman. Doesn't it bother you that your mother is dating him?"

Allison shrugged. "Why should it? They're both adults and my mom hasn't dated in a really long time either. Why shouldn't they have a little bit of fun together?"

"If you're okay with it, so am I."

"I'm going to go talk to Jason about this computer glitch, or whatever it is, and see if he's noticed anything on his," Allison said, as she stood and headed out the door.

~ Nine ~

"Did you have fun?" Allison and Stephen were having lunch when her mother and Captain came strolling into the casino.

"It was wonderful," her mother sighed dreamily. "We went to Vale and had dinner in the most fabulous restaurant that overlooked the whole valley. Then snow began falling, and I've never seen anything so beautiful."

"Captain, there's a problem..."Allison started, but Captain held up his hand to silence her.

"In a moment if you don't mind, Allison. We have something to tell you as soon as Jason gets down here."

"And I'm here," Jason announced and took a chair next to Stephen. "What is it?"

Allison noticed her mother appeared to be a little nervous, and even the Captain seemed nervous, but he grinned ear to ear.

"I know you will think this is sudden, and I suppose it is, but I've asked Trudy to marry me." He was nothing if not direct.

There was dead silence at the table. Allison's mouth hung open, but no sound came out. Jason and Stephen merely stared at their father. Captain and Trudy looked at each other and then at their respective children.

"You-you-asked my mother to m-m-marry you?" Allison stammered.

Marie McGaha

"He did and I've said *yes.*" Trudy held up her left hand that now sported a diamond engagement ring the size of a moon rock.

"Great," Stephen said, "this calls for champagne." He waved one of the waitresses over and ordered a bottle of very expensive French champagne.

"Congratulations, Captain. Congratulations, Trudy. Come here and let me kiss the bride." He leaned over the table and gave her a peck on the cheek. "Welcome to the family, *Mom*," he said, trying to relieve the tension at the table.

"Congratulations, Captain," Jason said. "Trudy, I'm very happy for you."

Stephen turned to Allison. "Well, I guess that makes you my sister."

Allison felt as if she was dreaming. "Marry him? You're getting married?"

"Allison, I thought you of all people would be happy for us. You told me you love Nelson like a father."

"I do, but I didn't expect you to marry him. Mother, you just met the man, how can you even consider marrying him?" She rose from the table. "Excuse me, I have work to do."

"I'll go after her," Trudy said.

"No, let me," Stephen volunteered. "She'll just get more upset if you try to talk to her now. She's pretty much mad at me already, so it won't

Marie McGaha

make much of a difference." He winked and left the dining room.

"I'm sorry, Nelson. I didn't think she'd react like that."

He wrapped an arm around her. "Don't worry. She'll get used to the idea."

"What if she doesn't?"

He shrugged. "She will. She's a strong girl. Don't worry about her. I'm sure Stephen will bring her around."

"Al, wait a minute." Stephen caught up to her quickly. "Al, will you just stop for a moment and listen to me?"

"Why? My mother is engaged to your father and she's only known him like two minutes."

"Shh, you don't need to shout where all the guests can hear." He took her by the arm. "Let's go to my office." Pulling her into the elevator with him, he pushed the button. Holding her hand all the way to his office, he told his secretary, "Take a long break, Julie. We need a few minutes alone." Then he pulled Allison to the inner office and locked the door.

"How can you be so calm about this?" Allison turned on him.

"Because I know that my father wouldn't have asked her to marry him if he didn't love her. He's nearly seventy years old, Al. I'm happy he's not going to be alone any more. And your mother has been

Marie McGaha

alone all of her life, how can you *not* be happy for them?"

Allison stared at him. After a long moment, she sighed. "I just can't imagine falling in love that quickly. It doesn't seem possible."

"Why not? There could be such a thing as love at first sight."

"*You* believe in love at first sight?"

He paused for a moment and looked at her. No, he wouldn't have said he believed in love at first sight even as recently as a week ago, but now as he looked into Allison's green eyes, he wasn't so sure. He shrugged.

"It could happen, and it has apparently happened for our parents. I think it's really immature of you to be throwing tantrums. You should be happy for them. You should be happy for your mother and be down there helping her plan the wedding, not up here acting like a child."

"I am not acting like a child, and I haven't thrown a tantrum in years." Her eyes flashed angrily at him as she stamped one foot with her fists ground firmly onto her hips.

Holding up his hands, he laughed. "I stand corrected." Then he closed the distance between them and held her face in his hands. "Look, Allison, I understand your reaction, but this isn't about you, darlin', it's about them. Now put a smile on that pretty face and let's go back downstairs and tell them how happy you are for them, okay?" She stared

Marie McGaha

straight ahead so he used his hands to move her head up and down in an affirmative motion.

She almost managed to hide the smile. "All right. Leave me alone." Looking up at him, her face still in his hands, their eyes met, and she felt heat lance through her body. Still as a statue, her eyes glued to his, she licked her lips. He lowered his mouth to hers and she didn't object, but she didn't help either.

Brushing his lips over hers, he could've sworn little electrical shocks sizzled between them. Her eyes were still wide open and he pulled back. She still hadn't pulled away and she hadn't told him to stop. He slanted his mouth over hers and his tongue slid between her lips. She opened her mouth and the kiss wasn't a sweet, romantic prelude, but a violent mating of two people who had held their passion far too long.

"If you're going to tell me to stop, do it now, Allison." His voice thick with desire.

She went very still beneath him, and then whispered, "Stop." Pushing against his chest, she stood. Moving away from her, he sat on the edge of the sofa as she smoothed her shirt and hair, but she wouldn't look at him.

"I'm going back down to congratulate my mother and your father," she said softly, and left him sitting there alone.

~ * ~

Marie McGaha

Stephen sat on the sofa and pushed a hand through his hair. Glad she'd stopped him, he didn't want their first time together to be in his office, and certainly not on a desk, but he still couldn't figure out why she refused him. The want in her eyes was clear, but what really floored him was that he'd never felt such passion before, such burning desire, and overwhelming need. Now he knew that he'd been in love with her for weeks, probably months, but he was just too dumb to figure it out.

Even though he hadn't been with another woman since the birthday girl had turned him down back in January, he hadn't really thought about it. However, since Allison had come to Biloxi, he'd been seeking her out and made sure he knew where she was at all times, not that he was stalking her, no, he just liked being near her, liked hearing her voice— even if it was just to hear her yell at him because he'd made her mad again.

He barged into her life as often as he could, joined her for lunch, usually uninvited, and stopped by her office with excuses to talk to her. He'd even maneuvered her out onto the beach that night so he could kiss her, which had only served to really screw things up, but he had gotten a kiss. Never had he acted like such a fool with a woman before in his life, and why should he? There was always another woman somewhere.

But now he didn't know what to do. He'd made a big deal out of making sure she knew he

Marie McGaha

would never be serious with a woman, and now he had discovered that he'd probably been in love with her all along.

Hadn't he felt jealousy when he found out she had lived with Wesley Smothers? And hadn't he felt like breaking something when he kissed her and she'd said Wesley's name? What was he going to do now? He couldn't very well tell her he'd suddenly changed his mind and he was in love with her. First, he needed time to sort it all out in his own mind, and then he'd worry about how to tell her. Of course, in the meantime, he still had to find out how she felt about him. Then he would just have to make sure she fell in love with him while he was figuring out how to tell her she was going to marry him. Grinning like an idiot as he thought about it, he finger-combed his hair, straightened his clothing and went back downstairs

Sitting down next to Allison, he asked, "Are you all right?"

"Yeah, yeah, just great," she replied dryly, as she watched Trudy and Captain gaze into each other's eyes as if they were both sixteen. The display was nearly more than Allison could take. What a day, her mother was getting married. She could hardly believe it. Love at first sight, indeed!

Allison cocked her head and looked at Stephen. He was much more subdued than usual. There had been a big change in him in just the few mo-

Marie McGaha

ments of time since she'd left him upstairs, but she didn't quite know what it was. There had been something in his eyes when he was kissing her, and she thought she could feel it when he touched her. She knew what was happening to *her* when he kissed her—she was scared to death and wasn't about to go any farther. Perhaps his new attitude was just regret over kissing her and he was embarrassed.

She had feelings for him, she'd had them for a long time, but she wasn't an immature girl. Having grown up rather quickly after the disaster named Wesley, Allison wasn't about to run headlong into anything—ever. Being in love with Stephen was definitely not in her plans. *In love with Stephen*, she thought. *I'm in love with Stephen?* But she hadn't planned on that little revelation to occur while she was sitting there watching her mother make out with her boss.

Looking at Stephen, she leaned close to him and whispered, "Forget about it, Stephen, it didn't mean anything."

Momentarily stunned, he just looked at her, but said nothing. *Didn't mean anything, huh?* Maybe not to her, but it meant something to him and he wasn't about to be in love alone. He'd never been in love before, and now that he was, he wasn't going to allow her to act like it meant nothing. Miss Allison Hamstead had no idea who she was dealing with.

"Mama, I want to apologize. To you too, Captain. I guess I was just a little... okay, a lot, shocked by your announcement. I want you both to know that I'm happy for you, and happy you've found each other," Allison told them.

"Thank you, baby," Trudy said with tears in her eyes.

"I knew you'd come around," Captain said. "I told you she was a smart girl, didn't I, darlin'?"

"Now that we've got that settled," Stephen said, "when's the wedding?"

"We don't see any reason to wait, so we thought we'd take a week off the first of next month and fly the whole family to Tahiti and have the wedding there. That is if no one objects?" Captain asked looking around the table.

"No, I don't think anyone does." Jason grinned and poured more champagne.

The rest of the afternoon was shot as far as going back to work, so Jason called Shelly and Janet and they all met for supper in the banquet hall and spent the rest of the evening celebrating. Allison and her mother made plans to go shopping for the perfect wedding dress, and Stephen and Jason made plans to take their father out for his bachelor party. Suddenly, Allison remembered the computer glitch she was going to mention to Captain, but with all the merriment, decided to wait until morning.

Marie McGaha

~ Ten ~

Allison called Captain the next morning when she came in to work, but he hadn't arrived yet. Even though her mother refused to move in with him until they were married, he sent the limo for her every morning so they could have breakfast together. Allison's nerves were wearing thin with both of them acting like teenagers. Captain was never where he was supposed to be and her mother did nothing but talk about the wedding and her dress and Allison's dress and Captain's tux and... Allison was going to scream if one more person mentioned the wedding.

Turning back to her computer, she went to work. At least she tried to go back to work, but the computer glitch was still glitching and the numbers were all wrong. She used a bad word, drank the last of her latte, picked up the phone, and dialed Stephen's extension, but his secretary said he wasn't in. *Where were all the men this morning?* She dialed Jason's number and although he was in, he was on a very important overseas conference call. Allison shook her head.

"What's the matter with you?" Stephen said, walking into her office.

"Thank goodness. I need you," she said.

He grinned. "Ah, the words I've been waiting to hear."

"Yeah, right. Look, I have a problem and I need help, but Captain isn't in, and Jason is busy..."

Marie McGaha

"You went to them first? I'm hurt."

"Stephen, I'm serious," she said.

So am I, he thought. "What's up darlin'?"

"This computer glitch. Everything is screwed up and I can't figure it out. None of the numbers are coming out right. Janet tried and got the same thing."

Stephen scooted her out of her chair and ran over the program. "When did this first happen?"

"I think it was the same day Captain and my mother got back, or maybe the day before, I don't remember, but I tried to tell him. He had an announcement to make, remember? And I haven't been able to get him cornered since," she said, sounding exasperated.

Stephen chuckled. "Yeah, he has been a bit like a teenager on his first date, hasn't he? I don't understand what's going on with this thing either."

"When it first happened it was the day I had come in really early, remember? While I was working, the computer blipped off and back on, and since then, I haven't been able to enter anything and make it come out right. It just doesn't match the hard copies. If we go by this, it looks like I've lost nearly eighty grand."

Stephen raised a brow. "Bought any new islands lately? Been to the Bahamas to open up any new bank accounts?"

Marie McGaha

She laughed. "Yeah, right. If I'd gone to the Bahamas with that kind of cash, I wouldn't have come back."

"So, Ms. Hamstead, you think of going to the Bahamas often?" He stood up and wrapped his arms around her.

Looking up at him, she asked, "What are you doing?"

"I was just thinking of you and me on an island, say Tahiti, next month? We can sneak away and find ourselves a nice, quiet stretch of beach and oh, I don't know, find some way to occupy ourselves."

"Are you out of your mind?"

"No," he smiled at her, "I'm not."

Holding her chin lightly, he slanted his mouth over hers, and slowly lowered his lips until they touched hers, and he felt the familiar sizzle pass between them. He couldn't believe Allison hadn't felt it as well, but she never said anything if she did. He took the kiss deeper, moved his hands around to the back of her head, and wrapped his fingers in her hair. Her hands came around his back and moved over him. She was like sliding into a warm bath, like coming home after a long trip, like having heaven on earth. Never had he known need, or desire, or passion like this. But now that he did, he could never give her up.

Marie McGaha

Allison sank into the kiss, and felt the warmth spread through her body clear down to her toes. She would never get used to the feel of this man, and knew he would never be old hat, never be casual. He would always feel like a dream to her, the one she would love, and the one she would equate forever with. This was the man she was made for, the one she was meant to love, and he was all she would ever want. The passion rose so quickly in her, Allison felt as if she had been hit with a brick. The feelings pulled her, pushed her, and assaulted her senses. Reality returned suddenly when the door opened and Janet walked in.

Freezing in position, their heads turned simultaneously to look at her. Janet's mouth hung open. "The door wasn't locked," she whispered. "I-I-I'll come back later." She backed out of the room and shut the door.

"Oh. My. Goodness." Allison turned thirteen shades of red.

"Well, that was fun," Stephen said and started laughing.

"It's not funny."

"Yes, it is."

"Stop laughing."

"Aren't we going to finish this?"

"Are you joking?"

"No. I'll pick you up at seven."

"For what?"

"Our date." He grinned.

Marie McGaha

"We have a date?"

"Of course we do," he said and kissed her quick, then left the office.

"What about my computer?" She called after him. "You didn't fix the computer."

After she smoothed her clothing and fixed her make-up, Allison dialed Janet's extension and asked her to come back. "I apologize, Janet, I... um, I am so sorry."

Janet laughed. "I am too. I will definitely knock next time."

"There won't be a next time. Stephen just, oh never mind."

"How long have you two been seeing each other?"

"We aren't," Allison said.

"Oh. I see." Janet looked at her intently. "You're in love with Stephen."

"No, I'm not. What would make you think something like that?"

"If it helps, I can see he really likes you, too." Janet grinned at the expression on Allison's face.

"How do you know?"

"Did you see the look on his face just a little while ago? I've known Stephen for a long time and I've never seen him look at a woman the way he looks at you. He's never even looked at a woman your size. Oh, I'm sorry, Allison, that was rude."

"Don't worry about it. I realize that I'm not exactly Stephen's type."

Marie McGaha

"What I meant to say was…"

Allison sighed. "Really, Janet. It's okay. I know I'm a big girl and men like Stephen fall in love with the super-model types. I learned my lesson in Chicago with a man like Stephen, it won't happen again."

"Please don't let my big mouth interfere…"

"No, stop now, it really is all right. I have a mirror. It's not a surprise to me that I'm fat."

Janet didn't know what to say to that, so she just left the office and shut the door quietly. Allison stared at the empty space and thought about what had just happened. She *was* a big girl and men like Stephen *didn't* look at women like her. So what was his angle? Why was he putting on such a show for her? Was he trying to feel better about himself? Have a fling with the fat girl and make her feel good about herself? Well, maybe she'd just see if two couldn't play that little game.

~ * ~

Finally home after a long day, Allison stripped and went into the bathroom. Running a hot bath filled with fragrant bath oils, she pinned her hair up, stepped into the water and sank up to her chin. *Oh, it feels so good.* She closed her eyes for a few minutes and then washed and shaved her legs. Spending a great deal of time on her appearance, she slathered herself in creams, lotions, and perfume. The exotic mixtures assaulted the senses in the subtlest

Marie McGaha

of ways with a blend of cinnamon, sandalwood, sage and opium oils.

Dressing carefully, she wore a pair of silk and lace panties, thinking of the expression on Stephen's face when he saw them. The black lace had silver threading and she bought them just for tonight. Her black dress was made from soft and silky jersey that hung in a cowl that dipped deep into her cleavage, clinging to her body, falling softly over her hips to below her knees, with a slit up one side to mid-thigh. Only thin straps covered her shoulders, and the back left her skin bare to her waist. Adding a pair of black lace thigh highs and a pair of strappy little heels that would have her feet aching by the time she was in bed, she only cared what Stephen would think when he saw her. Applying her make-up carefully, she then brushed her hair to one side and pinned it with a diamond-studded barrette her mother had given her for her twenty-first birthday.

Standing in front of the full-length mirror, she slowly spun in a circle. Smiling at her reflection, she was happy with what she saw. When she heard the knock at the door, she called out for Stephen to come in. She wanted to make a dramatic entrance, so she waited two beats after she heard the door open and shut. Then she walked into the living room with her beaded handbag held casually as if she always dressed this way and looked this stunning. Stephen stared as she spun in an achingly slow circle to allow him a view her from all angles.

Marie McGaha

Looking like he was going to drool, Allison smiled at him. "You like?"

He nodded. His mouth had gone dry and he forgot he actually spoke English. "We're staying in," he finally said.

"What?" She looked a little confused.

He cleared his throat. "I can't take you out dressed like that."

"Why not?"

"Because of all the marriages that will break up after the wives beat their husbands for staring at you. That and all the heads I'll have to break."

"I doubt that will be a problem," she said dryly.

Taking her hands, he kissed her softly. "You are absolutely gorgeous. I have never seen a woman more beautiful than you are, Allison. Thank you."

"For what?"

"For going out with me. For going to the trouble. For being so beautiful."

"Hmm, you keep that up," she whispered, "and I can almost guarantee you're going to get laid tonight."

"Is that a fact? Well then, I guess I should tell you that when I look at you I'm blinded by your beauty and I could spend forever gazing into your eyes."

"Wow, you're good." She kissed him.

"If you think that was good, you should see me with my clothes off."

Marie McGaha

"Oh, I plan to." She nibbled his ear lobe and ran her hands beneath his shirt over his smooth skin.

"Really, when do we start?"

"Right... after... you... take me to dinner like you promised."

"That's just wrong."

"I'll make it up to you later, I promise, but I'm starving."

"Okay, but I'm holding you to that."

"I'm counting on it."

Holding her hand as they walked to his car, Allison beamed at him when he opened the door for her and helped her inside. She wanted to just squeal out loud. Had she really just flirted shamelessly with the man she was in love with? Oh, it felt so good, and even better to be flirting with Stephen. Of course, she told herself, this is just a game, and no matter what her feelings for him were, or what they could be, she wasn't going to be anyone's fool again.

He took her to a nice restaurant and then dancing. They arrived back at his place sometime after one, and since she'd never been to his home before, she wasn't sure what to expect.

"Here we are," he said as he flipped on a light. "Home sweet home."

Allison looked around. A large brown leather sofa sat haphazardly in the middle of the living room, with no other furniture than a mega stereo system. "Decorate yourself?"

Marie McGaha

Stephen chuckled. "I'm not here that much really, but there's a garage for the 'Stang, and that was why I bought the house. And in here," he said, ushering her into the kitchen and dining room, "is the rest of the downstairs."

"You keep it light, don't you?" Allison asked as she looked at the empty dining room, and the pizza boxes covering the kitchen counters.

He shrugged. "No reason to fix it up. Come on."

Taking her hand, he led her upstairs. The only furniture in the bedroom was a massive bed that looked as if it could sleep ten all by itself. It actually had steps on either side to assist in getting onto it.

"Wow, that's a huge bed."

"You like it?"

"Yes, I do. It's wonderful."

"I was hoping you'd say that." He sat on the bed and patted the space beside him, so she sat beside him, though she was so nervous her mouth was dry and her heart pounded.

"You look beautiful," he said and leaned in to kiss her gently.

"Hmm, I bet you say that to all the girls," she said.

"Uh-uh. There's only you, Allison. Since I met you, there's been no one else. And you're the first woman I've ever had in this bed." He kissed her again.

Marie McGaha

He sounded so sincere, she almost believed him, but when he kissed her, she couldn't think of anything else. The only thing Allison could do was follow as he swept her along using his mouth and hands. She was caught up in the tidal wave of emotion and exquisite sensations flowing over her body. His hands moved over her as he started to undress her.

"Stephen," she said. "Turn off the light."

"No, Allison," he whispered hoarsely, "I want it on."

She pulled away from him. "Why?"

"I want to look at you." He tried to kiss her again.

"No," she said firmly. "I have to have the light off."

He stopped and looked into her eyes. "I don't understand."

"Look, I thought I could do this, but I can't. Please take me home."

He looked so frustrated, and then threw his arms up. "Fine."

They didn't speak the entire way back to her house, but when she started to open the car door, he put his hand on her arm. "I don't get it, Allison," he said. "I know you want me, and I want you. So why do you keep pulling back?"

She looked at him for a moment, and then shook her head. "Like you really don't know." Then she pushed the door open and got out. So did he.

Marie McGaha

"No, you're not running from me this time, Allison. You're going to tell me what your problem is."

"You," she shouted. "You're the problem. You don't have to do this, Stephen."

"Do *what*?" He ran up the front steps behind her. "Just what do you think I'm doing?"

She whirled on him. "This whole thing. Dating me, wanting to have sex with me. You've done your good deed, okay? The fat girl appreciates you showing her attention. Now, go back to your Twinkie girls." She pushed her front door open and tried to shut it in his face, but he was quicker than she was.

"You're really something, Allison. Maybe if you didn't spend so much time telling yourself what I'm like and started paying attention to what I'm *really* like, you would know I'm not doing anything to make the "fat girl" feel good about herself. I don't give a flying fig how much you weigh." With that, he left, slamming the door behind him. He was already squealing tires on the street in front of her house before Allison could make herself move from where she stood with her mouth hanging open.

"Oh my goodness," was all she could say as she sank to the living room floor and cried.

Marie McGaha

~ Eleven ~

Although Allison arrived late for work, Janet just smiled when she walked into her office. Blushing under the other woman's stare, Allison shut herself inside the room. After settling into her chair, she dialed Lynette and ordered a latte and cinnamon crunch bagel with hazelnut cream cheese. She was starving, well, not really, having already comforted herself the night before with a bag of Oreos, followed by a bag of mini-Milky Way bars, and topped that off with a banana covered in hot fudge and smothered in whipped cream. This morning she just wanted to forget the whole incident. Taking a deep breath, she forced a smile. *Okay Allison, things can't get any worse*, she thought.

At least not until her computer booted. The glitch she'd experienced before was still happening, but now, another twenty thousand dollars was missing. This was insane. Money did not just disappear all by itself, and since she was responsible for keeping everything in the right columns, she just couldn't understand what had happened. In a fit of frustration, Allison shouted at the machine in front of her just as Janet opened the door with her coffee and bagel.

"Does it yell back?"

"No, but I wish it did. At least I could ask what it's doing with all the money."

Marie McGaha

"Still not working right?" Janet set the food on the desk. "That's really strange. Have you talked to Captain about it yet?"

"I've tried," Allison slumped in her chair, "but it's so difficult to tie him down these days. You'd think my mother was the only woman on earth by the way he's acting."

"I think it's sweet," Janet replied, sitting in a chair in front of the desk. "And I hope that when I'm your mother's age, I find a man who will treat me the way Captain treats her. It's nice to know that growing old doesn't mean you can't still have a wonderful love life and be romantic."

"*Eeew!* Stop that, it grosses me out to think about my mother and Captain in, um, doing, um, well, you know. I know they do it, but I don't have to think about it."

Janet laughed. "It's no grosser than anyone else having sex."

"Oh, yes it is. She's my *mother*. I much prefer to believe that she only had sex once in her life and that was for the sole purpose of producing me," Allison said with a wry grin.

"I'll try to reach Captain for you and see what we can do about getting this computer fixed. I know Sam hired someone to install firewalls and other security measures, and they're all updated regularly. With all that in place, I can't imagine what the problem is."

Marie McGaha

"I know, but I can't do any work with it like it is. I'll have to do everything the old fashioned way, and then enter the numbers when the system is working properly." She sighed heavily. "Stupid machines anyway. I have to meet my mother downstairs at noon to go shopping... again. Would you give me a call so I don't forget?"

"No problem. Eat your bagel and drink your coffee, you'll feel better."

"Thanks." Allison sipped from the cup as Janet left the room.

Allison stared at the computer screen while she ate the bagel and drank the coffee. "No, it's more than a glitch," she mused aloud.

There was something going on that wasn't right and Allison spent most of the morning going back and forth through the program only to come up with the same numbers and the same problem time after time. The only thing to do was to pull the hard copies for the past six months and go over each report personally. *Oh great, that will take a week at least, probably longer*, she thought.

After wiping crumbs off her desk, she walked out of the office. It took her until noon to find all of the paperwork she needed. She made two trips to get the heavy boxes back to her desk and Janet reminded her she had an appointment with her mother to go shopping. Allison blew hair out of her face, picked up her purse, and went downstairs.

"Allison," her mother said, hugging her.

Marie McGaha

"Hey, Mama. How are you?"

"Oh," her mother said and actually blushed, "I'm just wonderful."

"You look wonderful, too." Allison smiled. "Let's go shopping."

Stopping for lunch first, Allison was still famished and ate like she was having her last meal on earth. Trudy looked at her daughter. She knew only too well Allison's behavior meant something was wrong. Allison always turned to food for comfort when she had a problem.

"What's the matter?"

With her fork frozen in mid-air, Allison glanced up. "I, um, what do you mean?"

"I know you well enough to see something is bothering you."

"Nothing is bothering me, Mama."

"Allison, does this have something to do with my getting married? I thought we had worked that out?"

Allison shook her head and covered her mother's hand with her own. "No, Mama. I'm happy you're getting married. You deserve every good thing you can get."

"Then what is it, baby?"

"Nothing. Let's just concentrate on you today."

"You sure?"

"Yes. Now finish eating so we can start shopping."

Marie McGaha

After lunch, the two women went to every bridal and lingerie shop in town, and Trudy bought a few things for the wedding night. Allison blushed as she watched her mother pick out see-through baby dolls and sheer negligees.

"Maybe I should try them on first," Trudy said, holding a red negligee in front of her.

"I don't think I need to see that," Allison commented with a chuckle.

"Oh, come on. I want your opinion."

Allison blew out a breath and shook her head. "Okay, Mama. Go try it on."

After Trudy had tried on the first few items, Allison got into the spirit of things and began picking out perfect wedding night surprises for the bride-to-be. As she picked up a negligee of satin and silk and held it in front of herself in the mirror, she wished she could wear something that sexy.

"The plus sizes are on those racks against the back wall," a sales lady said as she walked by.

"Excuse me?" Allison's mother turned around and grabbed the sales woman by the arm. "That was the rudest thing I've ever heard. You owe my daughter an apology."

"Mama," Allison said.

"No Allison, this woman is going to apologize to you."

"I didn't mean anything, really I didn't," the woman sputtered. "But I do apologize if I offended you."

Marie McGaha

"It's all right." Allison smiled.

"No, it's not," Trudy said and shoved all of the items she'd planned to buy at the woman as she grabbed Allison by the arm. "We'll be shopping elsewhere."

"Mama," Allison said as they walked out of the store. "You over-reacted."

"Maybe I did, but she was rude and I'm not going to allow anyone to be mean to my baby girl."

"It really doesn't bother me." Allison shrugged.

"It bothers me," Trudy said as they went into Victoria's Secret.

~ * ~

Back in her office, Allison moved the chairs out of the room and sat on the floor so she could go through the boxes of financial records. Beginning with the most recent and working backward, she had piles all over the floor. With a pen and pad of paper in her lap, she scribbled figures as she pulled papers out of the boxes. Allison was meticulous, always, so she knew her figures were correct. Even as a child, she was neat and orderly, and the habit had carried over into her schoolwork all the way through college. Her teachers had always complimented her, and made notes on her report cards, and her employers always had positive comments about her work. She could control all of those areas of her life, but she could never control her weight. Shrugging, Allison considered it a trade-off.

Marie McGaha

However, being that neat and meticulous had served her well, and especially now that she had all these figures to go over by hand. As she sat with the piles of papers all around her, the yellow legal pad in her lap, she knew she hadn't screwed up. She hadn't been able to go back far enough yet, but when she did, she knew there would be no discrepancy in her work. The problem was in the computer, and she didn't think there was a glitch either. Someone was siphoning off thousands of dollars from the casino and using her access code. What Allison didn't know was if someone was intentionally trying to make her look as if she was stealing from the casino, or if her access code had been the first one available to whoever was doing this. Her leg had fallen asleep, so she stood and stretched.

Just then the phone rang and Allison answered, "Yes, Janet?"

"Allison, there's a man here to see you."

"Thanks Janet, send him in." She replaced the receiver and hoped it wasn't Stephen. After the debacle she'd made out of their date last night, she didn't want to see him again so soon.

"Hi." The voice was familiar, but not Stephen's.

Allison whirled around. Staring at Wesley Smothers with her mouth wide open, Allison couldn't believe he was standing there. The nerve of him. He had been unfaithful, had broken every promise he'd ever made, then left her for her best friend. And

Marie McGaha

then he comes waltzing into her office as if he'd just seen her yesterday. The man had no shame.

"What are you doing here?"

"I came to see you. Kim told me where to find you."

"I'll remember to thank her later."

"Look, Allison, I know you're mad at me, and you have every right to be, but I came all the way down here to tell you I'm sorry."

Allison sat behind her desk. "And I'm supposed to throw myself at you now?"

"Sarah was a mistake. Everybody makes mistakes, Allison."

"Yes, I know," she said, looking him up and down so he didn't miss her meaning.

"What can I do to prove to you that I'm sorry, Allison? What can I say so you'll know I'm being sincere?" He stepped over the piles of papers until he stood beside her desk. "Allison, I still love you. I always have. I want us to work this out, baby."

Love? How dare he even mention the word to her? Wesley Smothers wouldn't know love if it fell on top of him, and here he was telling her he *loved* her. Pah-leese! How stupid and gullible did he think she was? Was she supposed to just drop everything, pack her suitcase, and follow him back to Chicago because he and Sarah were no longer together? Which she doubted was the truth anyway. Knowing Wesley, he and Sarah had probably had a fight and by tomorrow he'd be telling her the very same thing he was

Marie McGaha

now telling Allison. No, she wasn't buying any of this.

"Are you out of your mind, Wesley?" Allison looked at him as if he'd grown horns and turned purple. "You never loved me. You don't even know what love is."

"Allison, you aren't being reasonable..."

"Yes, she is," Stephen interrupted the conversation. He grabbed Wesley by the arm before the man knew what had happened and spun him around. "I'm the one who's not being reasonable," Stephen said and landed a hard right on Wesley's jaw that sent him flying backward into the wall. Then Stephen picked the man up and dragged him toward the door. Allison could hear Stephen ranting all the way down the hall, past Janet's desk to the main entrance. She ran to the door and peered down the corridor just in time to see Wesley stumble as Stephen pushed him into the hallway and then shut the main door firmly behind him. He came back to Allison's office and shut her door as well.

"Wesley Smothers?" Stephen asked. Allison nodded and bit her lip to hide the smile.

"What did you think you were doing, Stephen?" She asked without betraying any trace of the amusement she felt.

"Okay, I apologize," he finally said.

Her mouth twitched again. "You don't have to apologize."

Marie McGaha

"I should have asked you what you wanted first. You may have invited him for all I knew."

"I didn't." She sipped her tea.

"I know."

She did grin then. "How did you know?"

"I was coming to your office and saw him go in, so I waited and then, uh, well, I listened in the hallway." He grinned sheepishly.

"You did what? Stephen, how could you eavesdrop like that?"

"I'm sorry, Al. I know I shouldn't have, but I just had a feeling when I saw him that something wasn't right, and I didn't want anything to happen without me being here."

"Like what? What do you think could've happened?"

"I don't know. Men like that are creeps. He could've hurt you and then I would've hurt him." He looked at her and she knew he meant what he said.

"Thank you. Even though I don't want you cold-cocking everyone you see coming into my office, that one had it coming."

"You're not mad at me then?"

"No, I'm not mad at you. Wesley is an idiot and thought I'd just fall all over him because he said he was sorry and he loved me."

"That's the part that really lit my fire." He took her hand in his.

"When he said he loved me? Why?"

Marie McGaha

"Uh, I, well, it wasn't right for him to try to manipulate you like that after the way he treated you." He shrugged.

"He wouldn't know what love is if someone hit him over the head with it," she said. "But I really do have to get back to work, so if you'll excuse me." She withdrew her hand from his.

"Would you go out to dinner with me tonight?"

"I-I don't think that's such a good idea," Allison stammered.

"Just dinner, Allison, I promise. I'll take you home afterwards and I won't even come inside. I just want to spend some time with you."

Allison's heart wasn't beating normally as she thought about having dinner with him, though she finally nodded. "All right, but just dinner."

"I'll be back to pick you up at six," he said with a grin.

"I have a better idea," she said. "Tell me where you want to eat and I'll meet you there."

"Don't trust me?"

"Something like that."

He nodded and wrote down the name and address of the restaurant for her and left her to the piles of records all over the floor. She sighed and went back to work.

~ * ~

Marie McGaha

Arriving at the restaurant at six sharp, Allison saw Stephen had already arrived. When she got to the table, he held a chair for her.

"I'm glad you didn't stand me up," he said and flashed a grin.

"Why would I do that?"

He shrugged. "I don't know. Usually if a girl wants to meet you somewhere, there's a pretty good chance she's either not going to show up at all, or she's going to get a phone call about twenty minutes into the date that will give her the chance to leave if things aren't going well."

"*You've* been stood up?" She said it with such disbelief in her voice that Stephen laughed.

"Yeah, believe it or not, I've been stood up once or twice in my life."

"I don't believe it, but if you say so," Allison said as the server came to take their drink order.

Stephen picked up his menu and looked at Allison over the top. "What do you feel like eating?"

"I don't know," Allison mused as she looked at her menu.

"The seafood is good here," he suggested.

"The seafood is good everywhere in this town." Allison laughed. "But I think I'd like the salmon."

The server brought their drinks and took their dinner order. Stephen ordered for them both and smiled at Allison as the server walked away.

142

Marie McGaha

"Stephen," Allison said, drinking deeply from her appletini. "I think someone is stealing from the casino." She looked at him levelly.

"Why would you think that?"

"That's what the papers were doing on the floor of my office this morning. I pulled all the records for the last six months since I started working there, just to recheck everything, and my numbers are right. There are a few piles to look over, and I may have to pull the previous six months before I came to work as well, but there is something wrong. There's nearly a hundred thousand dollars missing that I can see right now."

He leaned across the table as far as he could and said in a low voice, "A hundred grand? Are you sure?"

She nodded. "Of course I'm sure. And whoever's doing it is using my access code."

"Why didn't you tell me earlier?"

"You were busy punching Wesley, and I haven't seen you since then."

"Okay, first thing in the morning you show me what you've got and I'll get my hands on my father one way or the other. We're supposed to leave for Tahiti in three days. I'd like to get this taken care of before we go. It's probably nothing. We have the best high-tech security on those computers. It's practically impossible to hack into them."

"The operative word is 'practically', but not *completely* impossible. For every security system

Marie McGaha

produced, there is somebody out there figuring ways to get around them, or through them. We might want to wait until after the wedding to talk to Captain, I don't want anything to ruin the big day. There's a lot of paperwork to go over. I can show you in the morning. I also want to see the deposit records and the individual table receipts as well. There is the possibility I'm wrong and it really is a glitch."

"But you don't believe it's a glitch, do you?"

She inhaled and blew the breath out before answering. "No, I don't."

Marie McGaha

~ Twelve ~

Allison watched as the computer tech looked at her computer. His name was Greg. Sam Jones, head of security for the casino, had hired him to install the security systems in all of the casino's computers. He was currently reviewing those systems, attempting to figure out what had happened with Allison's computer. Apparently, none of the other computers had been affected, and he had been working for the better part of an hour in Allison's office. Finally, he turned toward her and smiled. "I found the problem and fixed it. You may have to re-enter some data that was lost, but everything should be good to go."

"Really? It was just a glitch then?"

"It looks that way." He smiled again and went toward the door.

"Thank you, I appreciate you coming in." She watched him leave and went back to her computer. Sighing, Allison knew it was going to take a full day to get everything straightened out again, and she would be working very late tonight. Calling Lynette, she ordered a latte before getting to work. An hour later, Janet knocked on the door.

"Come in," Allison replied without looking up.

"I have the bank records you asked for." Janet said, setting the files on the desk.

"Thanks." Allison spun around in her chair and flipped the folder open.

Marie McGaha

"What do you think you're going to find?"

"Hopefully, nothing, but I want to make sure everything is right."

"Greg told Sam everything was fixed and it was a glitch," Janet said.

"And I'm sure he's right. This is just for my own peace of mind." She looked up and smiled.

"Okay, let me know if you need anything else," Janet said and left the room.

Allison read over the first page and turned back to the computer. She spent the rest of the afternoon with her head bent over the desk staring at the computer screen.

"Hey," Stephen said, sticking his head in the door, "are you going to work all night?"

She looked up and smiled. "I didn't realize I'd worked so late. What are you doing?"

He grinned as he walked into the office and shut the door. He bent over her and made her tip her head all the way back to look at him. "I thought I'd come by and make sure everything was taken care of with your computer. And to make sure you don't work all night."

"I'm leaving in a minute," she said and began shutting the computer down.

"So tell me why you're still going over financial records when the system has been fixed?" Stephen asked while they walked down the hall to the stairs together.

Marie McGaha

"Because I'm anal," Allison told him with a laugh. "I just can't drop something once I get started. If I don't go through the records and finish what I started, I'll drive myself crazy thinking I screwed something up. Especially if it still doesn't come out right in the end."

"I'm sure everything is fine. No one has ever stolen from the casino since we've been here in Biloxi, so I doubt anything is irregular now."

"You're probably right, but if I don't follow through, I'll never get any sleep."

"You go right ahead and be anal then," he said with a laugh. "How about going with me to grab some pizza?"

"Hmm." Thinking about it for a moment, she said, "All right, I'll go with you for pizza."

"Then you can go home with me," he said matter-of-factly.

"Stephen."

"Boy, you are anal aren't you? I'm teasing you, Allison."

She looked at him for a moment and bit her bottom lip. "Okay. I'm sorry, it's just that..."

"You don't trust me?"

She nodded her head. "Of course I don't trust you."

Stephen laughed as he held the door of his truck for her, and when he saw her give the old beater a second look, he explained, "The Mustang is only for serious dates. This old Chevy is for pizza."

Marie McGaha

Allison laughed as she climbed in. They drove to Pizza Hut and ordered a pizza with everything, including the cheesy, twisty crust and marinara sauce. He took her out for an ice cream cone afterward and they walked on the beach as they ate.

"I love this place," Allison said.

"You don't miss Chicago?"

"No, it wasn't the place for me, and I missed the ocean so badly. Lakes just don't take the place of an ocean. How about you? Do you miss Nevada?"

"Not at all. I hate the desert." Stephen took her hand as they walked together.

"That's what southern California is too, a great big desert with millions of people and miles of concrete. There's an ocean, but I don't miss L.A. at all. This feels like home to me and now that my mama will be living here, it's even better."

"Are you ready to go to Tahiti?"

"I've never been there, so it's going to be great. I can hardly wait. You've been there already?"

"A couple of times." He nodded. "Captain was big on vacations when I was a kid. Besides, most of the trips could be written off as a business expense, so we got to go to a lot of cool places. Are you ready to go home?"

"Yeah, I guess we better since I have to get up early. I still have to pack."

They walked hand-in-hand back to Stephen's truck and when he pulled onto Beach Boulevard, he asked, "Are you sure you want to go to *your* home?"

Marie McGaha

Allison looked at him and thought about it. No, she didn't want to go home, she wanted to go with Stephen, she wanted to feel his hands on her and she wanted him to kiss her. "Yes," she said, but she shook her head no.

He chuckled, squeezed her hand, and said, "When you know for sure what you want, let me know."

"I will," she said with a smile.

"I'll be by in the morning," he told her.

He dropped her at her car in the casino parking lot and waited until she was inside, and she waved as he drove off. Allison watched him as he left the parking area and thought he was definitely persistent in his pursuit of her, and she was thinking more and more, that just maybe, it was time to let him catch her. Tahiti might just be the place to do it.

Turning to look out the rear window to make sure the way was clear, she saw an SUV pull up, blocking her, and thought the driver must be waiting for a parking spot. When Sam, head of security, jumped out of the passenger seat, she waved as he walked to her car.

Rolling down the window, she said, "Hey, Sam. What's up?"

"Not much, Allison. Going home?"

"Yeah, I've got to pack for the trip tomorrow," she told him.

Marie McGaha

"All by yourself here tonight, huh? I expected Stephen to be with you."

She laughed. "I guess we are together a lot, but he just dropped me off if you're looking for him. I expect he'll be back at his place in a few minutes if you want to call him at home. He probably has his cell on him though."

Sam suddenly opened the car door and grabbed her around the throat as he dragged her out of the car. Allison grasped his wrists with both hands, as he dragged her kicking across the pavement. He was too strong for her, and she felt herself blacking out. The last thing she saw was a second man she vaguely recognized, who opened the door of the SUV.

Allison came to a few minutes later, her hands and feet bound, and there was a gag over her mouth. The SUV traveled at a high rate of speed and she didn't have a clue why Sam would risk his job, his position with the casino, or his entire life to kidnap her. Only knowing Sam on a casual basis, Allison thought they had been on friendly terms. What she could have done to make him go to this length, she couldn't fathom. Perhaps he was after Stephen and holding her hostage was the way to get to him. But Stephen had never mentioned any problems between himself and Sam, so that didn't make any sense either. Her mind whirled, trying out every scenario she could possible fathom and nothing made sense.

Marie McGaha

Lying on the seat for nearly two hours, her hands and feet were numb. The SUV slowed down and made a hard right onto what was either a dirt road or a badly damaged paved road, because it bumped and jarred her as the tires dipped into deep holes and bounced back out. She became nauseous and wished they would hurry up and get to wherever they were going so she could sit up before she vomited.

Allison guessed another fifteen minutes had passed when the vehicle came to a stop. Sam opened the door and pulled her upright. He and the other man, who she now recognized as Greg, the computer tech, carried her into a building. Setting her on a dirty sofa, dust puffed up in the air from her weight, as Sam removed the gag and Allison sneezed.

"Sam, what are you doing?"

"I'm sorry, Allison. I didn't want it to be this way, but you just wouldn't leave well enough alone."

She looked at him, confused at his meaning. "I don't understand, Sam. What are you talking about?"

"Allison, don't play stupid. How many people know about it?"

"Know about *what*? You aren't making any sense."

151

Marie McGaha

Greg leaned over so he was face-to-face with her. "The money, sweetheart. Is that simple enough or do you want pictures?"

Allison leaned back, he was too close, and she didn't like it. Furrowing her brow as she thought about what he said, she gasped. The only money she knew about was... *oh my goodness!* They were talking about the nearly hundred grand she'd found missing on the computer.

"The computer glitch? It wasn't a glitch, was it? You've been stealing from the casino."

"See, I knew she was smart," Greg said sarcastically. "I told you we should've just taken what we had and gotten out of there. You're just too greedy."

Sam nodded. "Allison, why didn't you just drop it? We wouldn't have had to do things this way if you'd just let it be."

"I still don't understand, Sam. Why kidnap me? Why not just take the money and go anyway?"

Sam shook his head. "I hate doing this, Allison. I always liked you, but when you discovered that money missing, I thought you'd just think it was a glitch, and once I brought Greg in to fix it, you'd drop it. But you requested the bank records then and all the past records. I knew it wouldn't take you long to figure out I've been siphoning off money from the casino for nearly five years now. I've stolen nearly two million dollars and that was all I was going to take. As soon as we hit the two million mark, we

Marie McGaha

were going to disappear. But you just wouldn't let it go."

"You and Greg were going to run off together?" *Man*, she thought, *that was weird.*

Sam grinned guessing what she was thinking. "No, Greg was just a means to an end."

"Hey, I'm your *partner*," Greg reminded him. "Half the cash is mine."

"No, it's not." Sam shook his head, pulling a gun from his jacket pocket, and firing one shot into Greg's forehead. Allison didn't know if she screamed or not, because she couldn't breathe with her heart in her throat.

"Don't worry, Allison. We have other plans for you," he said, putting the gun back in his pocket. She couldn't quit staring at the body on the floor. Finally, Sam picked up the other end of the sofa and moved the whole thing in a half circle so she faced the other direction.

"Wh-wh-what do you mean?"

"You see," a familiar voice behind her said. Allison twisted her head around to see Janet walk toward her. "We are taking the money and going away together. And you, boss lady, will be left to take the rap. See, it's going to look like you and Greg there cooked up the whole thing and then you turned on him. You'll go to prison for a very, very long time."

Marie McGaha

"That's crazy. No one will believe it. When you and Sam don't show up for work, they're going to know."

"No." Janet shook her head. "We aren't leaving until after everyone finds out about you. Then Sam will quit his job because he will feel so guilty for not protecting the casino from you, and I'll quit because I'll be so distraught over the whole situation. After all, you and I have become so close over the past few months. My dear cousin, Nelson will understand.

"Of course, an added bonus for us was your mommy coming along and duping Captain into believing she loved him, and of course, they'll all believe she was in on it. Even though they won't be able to prove it, I'm sure Captain will send her packing right back to California."

"You'd better leave my mother out of this or you'll be laying right there along with your buddy." Allison rarely lost her temper, but bringing her mother into this did it. Janet simply smiled, walked out of the room and got into the SUV.

"Look Allison, I really wanted you to leave this alone and not get involved. We had a way to put it all off on Greg until you started sticking your nose in where it didn't belong. I'm going to leave you here for a while. You'll be fine. No one comes around this place anymore. I'll be back in a while to turn you loose. After all, they can't find you tied up or this will never work."

Marie McGaha

Allison leaned back against the sofa and rested her head. This was so freaking weird, she couldn't get her mind around it. Nothing made sense to her. Surely they didn't believe Captain would take their word that she was involved? Stephen wouldn't believe something like that about her, would he? Jason would know she didn't have anything to do with stealing from the casino, wouldn't he?

Shifting her bottom around until she could lift her legs, she managed to put them up on the sofa. Tired and still feeling a little sick to her stomach, she needed to rest. Her mother would miss her in a few hours and would call her cell phone, which was still in her car. And when she didn't answer, her mother would call Stephen's cell phone. Stephen would know something was wrong. She hoped he would anyway. And even if he didn't at first, wouldn't he check the garage where he'd dropped her off? When he found her purse and keys still in the car, he'd call the police. All she had to do was wait. Hearing a noise behind her, she jumped, then turned slowly around and saw Greg's arm move. He wasn't dead, but he would be if someone didn't find him soon.

"Greg, can you hear me?"

He moaned.

"Greg, move you arm if you understand me."

He moved his arm.

Marie McGaha

"Okay," she said, exhaling heavily. He was alive and coherent. Mostly. "Do you have a cell phone?"

He moved his arm again.

"Okay, I'm going to try to get to you and I'll use the phone to call for help."

He didn't move. Allison swung her feet off the sofa onto the floor, and scooted to the very edge of the cushion, sliding to the floor. She moved like an inchworm over the scarred wood. Her arms had fallen asleep and she felt dizzy, but she kept going until she reached Greg. Blood from his head formed a pool, soaking her clothing as she maneuvered herself along what seemed an endless expanse.

With her hands bound tightly behind her back, she was just too big to get her knees and feet through to have them in front of her. Trying another tack, she scooted and twisted until she positioned herself with her back to Greg. With her bound hands at his waist, she felt with her fingers, trying to reach into his front pants pocket to locate the cell phone. The awkward position made it impossible to lift him up enough to reach the pocket. She began shaking him as hard as she could.

"Greg. Are you still with me?" She waited, but he didn't move. "Greg!" She shouted at him and heard a faint moan. "Greg, wake up. I can't get to your phone. You have to help me. Greg. Help me find your phone."

Marie McGaha

He moved, so she moved closer to him and felt the hard line of the phone in his pocket. She still couldn't get her hands far enough inside the pocket to reach it, so she tried inching it up toward the top of his pocket from the outside. Finally, it began to move. Her hands had little feeling left in them because of the lack of circulation, but she was finally able to inch the phone out of his pocket. Scooting away from Greg, she laid the phone on the floor and managed to flip it open, and then scooted around so she could see the numbers. Using the tip of her tongue to hit the emergency button, Allison sighed with relief as she heard the familiar sound of dialing. Allison laid her head on the phone, and finally heard a voice answer.

"Hello, hello! Yes, I'm, I'm," she sobbed. "Please help me! We need an ambulance and the police."

"Do you know your location, ma'am?"

"No, I've been kidnapped, and I don't know where I am. Please, please help us! They shot Greg and there's blood everywhere. Hurry, please!"

"Don't hang up, ma'am. Stay on the line until I can get help to you. Are you hurt?"

"No, just Greg. He's been shot, he's hurt. He might be dead, I don't know."

"Just stay calm, okay? I've got the police on the way. We're using the GPS in the phone to get a location on you, so don't hang up."

"Okay, okay. Just please, please hurry."

Marie McGaha

"We're trying ma'am. Just stay calm."

"I'm trying," she sniffled. Allison tried hard not to cry, but it seemed as if an eternity passed before the 9-1-1 operator had any good news for her.

"Ma'am, we have a location on you and the police are on the way, but I'm going to stay on the line with you until they arrive."

"Th-thank you," Allison said. An interminable amount of time seemed to pass before she finally heard sirens. "I can hear the sirens. Thank you so much. I can hear them."

"Okay, but don't hang up yet. I want to make sure they have a visual on you before you hang up."

"Okay," Allison cried. The sirens came closer and closer, and then stopped. She heard car doors and then the sound of a man shouting.

"This is the police, is anyone in there?"

"Yes, I'm here," Allison tried to shout.

"Are you alone?"

"No, um, yes, well, Greg is here but he's been shot. Please hurry." Then a dozen policemen with guns drawn, rushed into the building, and she began to cry again.

"Put your weapons away," one of the cops told the other men. "Get the stretcher in here, we've got a GSW," he said into the mike on his collar. He began cutting the tape from Allison's wrists and ankles. "Do you know who is responsible for this ma'am?"

Marie McGaha

She nodded. "He is. He and Sam kidnapped me, but Sam shot him and left with Janet. They were going to frame me for it. Sam is supposed to be back, you've got to tell Captain." The officers looked at each other, she wasn't making any sense to them.

"She needs to go to the hospital," Lt. Aubrey told the other man.

"I need to call my mom. I need to call Stephen. They'll tell Captain," Allison continued rambling, making no sense to the officers.

"Come on, Miss. We're going to take you to County Memorial and have a doctor look at you. We'll have someone from forensics meet you there, too. We have to process you for evidence."

"Where am I?" Allison looked at them as they loaded her onto a gurney.

"You don't know where you are?"

She shook her head. "No, they dragged me out of my car and blindfolded me."

"You're in the swamps not far from New Orleans. Where did they kidnap you from?"

"My job in Biloxi." Her head was beginning to hurt. "Can you please call my mother and tell her to call Stephen? They need to know what's going on. Stephen will call Captain."

"Who's this Captain you keep talking about?"

"Stephen's father. My mother's fiancé." She lay back heavily on the gurney as the EMT's loaded her into the ambulance. "What about Greg?"

Marie McGaha

"He didn't make it. I'm sorry."

She shook her head. "It's okay, I didn't know him." But she began crying again anyway.

The ambulance ran all the way to New Orleans without sirens and pulled into the emergency room bay. Attendants pulled the gurney out and took Allison inside, where she was met by a nurse who began asking her questions and taking vital signs. Allison tried to tell them she was fine. The blood flow had returned to her hands and feet, and except for a slight case of nausea and a headache, she was fine. The forensics officer processed her hands and feet and took her clothing. After swabbing her cheek for DNA, the technician also cut some of Greg's blood from her hair. Allison felt as if hours passed before the female officer finished and finally left.

The doctor came in looking at the notes the nurse had made and smiled at her. "I'm Dr. Kline, how are you Allison?"

"Tired, but fine."

"We got the test results back and you appear healthy and no worse for wear considering what you've been through."

Allison closed her eyes. "I've been under a lot of pressure lately and my mother is getting married... oh no, we're supposed to leave for Tahiti in the morning. What time is it?"

"A little after one in the morning," he answered.

Marie McGaha

The nurse came in then, followed by Stephen, Trudy, and Captain. "You have some visitors," she said brightly.

"Allison!" Her mother hugged her tightly to her breast and both began to cry. "Are you all right, baby?"

"I'm fine, Mama," Allison sniffled.

"Come on Trudy," Captain said, "let me in there." He caught Allison up in a bear hug and squeezed until she pounded him on the back.

"I can't breathe," she gasped.

Captain released her, but held her hand. She looked at Stephen and began to cry again. He open-ed his arms and she fell against his chest. Holding her close, he kissed the top of her head, and glanced up at his father, then at Trudy. Captain put his arm around Trudy and walked her back to the waiting room.

"Oh, Stephen," Allison continued crying. Wiping the tears from her cheeks, he smiled. "Are you all right, Al? I mean really all right?"

She nodded and then shook her head. "I don't know. I'm not hurt really, but they scared the crap out of me, and I watched Sam kill a man and Janet, oh my, did they tell you about Janet?"

He nodded. "We got the whole story out of them. Janet blubbered and blamed everyone but herself, and Sam blamed Janet and Greg. They're both in jail right now. There's so many charges

Marie McGaha

against them, neither one will ever get out of pris-on."

"I'm sorry," Allison said and started to cry again.

"You've got nothing to be sorry for. I should have taken you seriously when you told me you didn't think it was a glitch. If I had believed you, and helped you look into it further, none of this would've happened. If anyone has anything to be sorry for, it's me. And not just that, I'm sorry I never told you how much you mean to me, and I never told you," he tipped her face up to his, "that I love you, Allison. I never knew how much until I got that phone call. I have never known such abject fear in my life. And when I talked to the cops, and realized how very easily you could have been lying there dead with Greg, I—I can't imagine what my life would be without you." He leaned toward her and kissed her. She wrapped her arms around him and kissed him as if it was the last kiss they'd ever share.

"I love you, too," she whispered.

"You do?" He pulled back and looked into her eyes and she nodded.

Stephen felt his knees wobble, and he braced his hands on either side of Allison's legs. Lowering his forehead to her shoulder, he took a few deep breaths. He raised his head, looked into her eyes and smiled. Slanting his mouth over hers, he kissed her deeply.

Marie McGaha

~ Thirteen ~

Allison took the abduction as if it was no big deal, or at least she hoped to appear that way. Stephen constantly hovered over her as if she would suddenly disappear when he looked away. Though she tried to take that in stride as well, to tell the truth, it was harder on her than the kidnapping and murder had been. Even though they said they loved one another, Allison's many emotions overwhelmed her. She needed some space, and now things were more strained between them than before, because she pulled back, and Stephen acted as if they were a couple.

Allison didn't want to hurt his feelings, and she truly did love him, but being kidnapped wasn't enough of an excuse to change her mind. Not only that, she still couldn't push past what Wesley had done. Knowing it wasn't fair to Stephen, Allison wasn't going to allow her heart to be broken by another handsome man. A man like Stephen, who was more than handsome, was capable of thrilling her more than she ever thought possible, and was just as capable of ripping her heart out. No, she'd never allow that to happen again. Sometimes love just wasn't enough. So Allison kept the wall up between them, and no matter how he tried, she couldn't, wouldn't, allow him to get any closer.

~ * ~

Marie McGaha

The air was balmy when they arrived on the island of Tahiti, and the waiting limo took them to their hotel where they were shown to their rooms. Allison squealed when she saw the rooms were actually little huts spread out on a private beach. She'd never seen anything like it and wrapped her arms around Captain in a tight hug.

"Oh, how have I lived without seeing this before?"

"I'm glad you like it." He chuckled at her enthusiasm.

"Mama, is your room just like this?"

"Yes, we all have the same accommodations." Trudy smiled at her daughter.

She had never been so scared in her life when her baby girl couldn't be found, nor so relieved when she'd gotten the phone call saying Allison was in the hospital in New Orleans, and thankfully, uninjured. After Trudy found out what had happened, Captain had barely been able to keep her from killing Janet and Sam. Now they were all together in Tahiti, and she wasn't going to let anything keep them from having a good time.

Trudy and Captain went off to their own hut and Jason and Shelley went to theirs. That left Allison and Stephen standing in front of Allison's room.

Allison opened the door, and said, "I guess I'll see you for supper."

Marie McGaha

"I guess so." Stephen kept his hands in his pockets as he walked away.

Allison found the room well equipped, and even though it looked like something from Robin Crusoe on the outside, the inside was quite modern. The only modern conveniences missing were a telephone and television, which she didn't mind at all. The bathroom even had a Jacuzzi tub, and a crank on the wall allowed the roof to be rolled back to reveal an open sky. She couldn't wait to sit in the tub and gaze at the stars. Opening the back door, she was greeted by an expanse of beach with sand as white as snow and fine as sugar. Unable to resist taking a few steps to see if it was as soft as it looked, she found that it was. The ocean beyond was so blue, her eyes hurt to look at it. Everything was so wonderful, Allison didn't think the week they'd have here would be enough time at all.

After showering, she dressed for dinner and met the other members of the family at the main hotel for dinner. Afterward, they all strolled along the village streets and browsed. They took pictures, acting like tourists, and when they stopped at a street café, everyone ordered tropical drinks served in coconut shells with little umbrellas in them and laced with lots of rum. But Allison noticed Trudy ordered peach iced tea instead. Allison thought her mother didn't look well as the others laughed and talked. When Trudy excused herself to go to the ladies room, she followed her.

Marie McGaha

Allison pushed the door open, and heard her mother retching inside one of the stalls, she hurried inside. Wetting some paper towels in the sink, she passed them under the stall door and waited until her mother came out.

"Mama, are you all right?"

"I'm fine, baby. It's just the heat." She washed her face and rinsed her mouth.

Allison rubbed her mother's back. "Mama, it gets hotter than this in California and you never got sick before."

"Then it must be the humidity," she said with a smile that didn't quite convince Allison.

"It's humid in Mississippi," Allison countered. "Tell me what's wrong. Are you sick? Have you come down with something?"

Trudy laughed and shook her head. "Yes, I've come down with something. You're going to be getting that baby brother or sister you've always wanted."

Allison almost fell down. "Are you sure?"

Trudy nodded. "I've been to the doctor and I'm due the end of February."

"Oh my..."Allison stopped. She began to laugh and Trudy looked at her.

"It's not that funny. I know I'm old, but it's not unheard of for a woman my age to have a baby. I read just the other day that the number of woman having babies after forty is increasing all the time."

Marie McGaha

"Uh, I don't know what to say, Mom. What did Captain say?"

"Oh, Allison. I..."

Just then, Shelly walked in. "Is everything all right in here?"

"Um, sure, sure it is," Trudy said weakly and wouldn't look at Allison or Shelly.

"Okay," Shelly said. "Which one of you is pregnant?"

"It's definitely not me," Allison said, looking at her mother.

Shelly looked at each of them. "Are you serious?"

They both nodded.

"What did Captain say?"

"I just asked her that and she didn't answer me. What *did* Captain say, Mama?"

Trudy took a deep breath. "I haven't told him."

"What?" Allison and Shelly said simultaneously.

"Mama, how could you not tell him before you marry him?"

"Trudy, he has to know. You can't keep this from him," Shelly said.

"I know, I know, but there was so much going on and I didn't even realize I could be pregnant until a few weeks ago. I'm forty-three years old, and my last baby is nearly twenty-four, so why would I even think I was pregnant? Especially with Captain being,

well, he's nearly seventy. He's very, um, vigorous."
She smiled when the other two women frowned.
"But I never thought he could get me pregnant."

"You have to tell him tonight," Allison said.

"I know and I will. I promise."

~ * ~

Stephen found Allison sitting on the beach in
the moonlight after everyone came back from the
night out.

"Okay, out with it." Stephen looked at Allison.

"Out with what?" She asked innocently.

"Whatever it is you're thinking about so hard
over here by yourself." He sat down beside her.

"My mother's pregnant," she said flatly.

"Whoa, whoa, whoa! What? What do you
mean she's pregnant? And how does she plan on ex-
plaining that to my father?"

Allison's face lost all humor when she glared
at him. "What does that mean? And you'd better be
very careful with your next words." She stood with
her hands on her hips, looking at him, challenging
him.

Taking a deep breath, Stephen reassessed the
situation before he spoke. He didn't want to fight
with her, but the fact was, her mother was pregnant
and marrying his father like everything was... no, it
just wasn't possible. Was it? His mind spun so fast he
felt a little dizzy. Stephen remained sitting, looked
quite stunned, and then looked up at Allison. He

Marie McGaha

cleared his throat twice before he could make a sound. "Are you," he cleared his throat again, "are you saying my *father*... how?"

Allison covered her mouth with her hand to hide the fact she was laughing. "I think they did it pretty much the same way most people do." She sat back down. "Did you think they were going to get married and not have sex?"

He shrugged. "I thought perhaps they'd have sex a few times, but it never occurred to me that he could, could... you know, get her pregnant. He's seventy for Pete's sake."

"And my mother is forty-three. Believe me, I never thought I'd be getting a brother or sister out of this relationship either, but it is kinda cool. Just think, you and I will share a sibling."

Stephen rolled his eyes. "What did my father say when she told him?"

"That's the thing. She hasn't told him, but she's going to tonight. Shelly and I talked to her. The whole age thing you know. But she promised to tell him, so I suppose we'll find out in the morning what he thinks."

"I hope he doesn't have a stroke or something," Stephen said, only half kidding.

"I think he'll be fine." Allison patted his leg.

"How do you feel about it?" He held her hand in his and grinned.

"Oh, I don't know. It seems kind of strange that my mother is having a baby at her age, but I

Marie McGaha

guess I'll get used to it. I've always wanted a baby brother."

"Believe me," Stephen said dryly, "it's not all it's cracked up to be."

Allison laughed. "You don't know what you'd do without Jason."

"Yeah, maybe, but I'd give it a shot."

"Hey, we've got to get up early in the morning," Allison said. "Tomorrow's the big day."

~ Fourteen ~

"Allison." Stephen held her hand. "I was hoping we could talk a little while."

"What about?"

"About what happened at the hospital," he said.

"I don't know what you mean." She looked away from him.

"You said you loved me, Allison. I told you I love you, and you said you love me, too. But since then, you haven't given me a moment alone with you."

"Look, Stephen, I had been through a lot that night. I'd been kidnapped, seen a man murdered, and found out that the woman who answered my phones was plotting against me. If I said I loved you, it was just in the broadest sense of the word."

"So, when I told you I love you, did you think I was using it in the broadest sense of the word as well?" He was trying hard not to let the anger he felt creep into his voice.

"I-I just thought it was one friend to another." She refused to look at him even though she could feel his eyes on her.

"What do you want from me, Allison?"

"Nothing. What makes you think I ever wanted anything from you, Stephen?" Turning toward him, she said, "You're the one who's been pursuing me, not the other way around, so don't try to put this on

171

Marie McGaha

me." She got to her feet and started back to her bungalow.

Stephen caught her by the arm. "So, this means nothing to you? *I* mean nothing to you, is that right, Allison?"

"I didn't say you mean nothing. I value our friendship, Stephen, but it's never going to be more than that. Ever. So go find yourself another play-mate, all right?" She glared at him and he released her arm.

Leaving Stephen standing there alone wasn't easy, but she just couldn't trust him, or herself, and she wasn't going to take the chance with Stephen that she had with Wesley. She wished she could ex-plain it to Stephen, but how could a man like that understand heartbreak? Yeah, he said someone had stood him up, but that was hardly the same thing. He had never loved a woman, had never trusted a woman, and he had never had one use him and hurt him the way Wesley and Sarah had hurt her.

She turned off the lights, turned over on her side, buried her face in her pillow and cried. As bad-ly as she wanted to tell Stephen she lied, she just couldn't bring herself to tell him she was in love with him. She loved him so much she ached to have him touch her. And watching her own mother have the life she wanted for herself was making her mis-erable. After crying herself out, she went to sleep.

Suddenly, someone pounded on her door. Alli-son looked at her watch and couldn't believe anyone

Marie McGaha

was awake at that hour. Pushing back the covers, she went to the door and found her mother, Captain, Jason, Shelly, and Stephen all looking at her.

"Oh, go away," Allison said, and went back to bed. "It's too early for this."

"Didn't you sleep well last night, baby?" Her mother sat on the bed beside her.

Captain sat on the other side. "You're about to become my daughter, so get out of bed and hop-to, young lady." She glared at him and he laughed. "Look, we're going to breakfast, so meet us up there. By the way, I know you already know this, but I'm going to be a father."

"And you're good with it?"

"Good with it? Of course I am. I'm on cloud nine, girl. I'm nearly seventy years old and I'm marrying that sweet young thing you call *Mama,* and I've knocked her up. You bet I'm good with it. I'm the happiest man in the world. Now let's go. On deck, matey!"

"Oh no, kill me now," Allison moaned and covered her head.

"You've only just started putting up with this," Jason informed her. "Get back to me when you've done it twenty-seven years."

"Please tell me you'll shoot me first?"

"No way," Shelly piped up. "If we have to suffer, so do you."

"Great. Now go away."

Marie McGaha

"Okay baby," Trudy said. "We'll meet you in the restaurant." Then it was suddenly and wonderfully silent.

Allison exhaled and shook her head as she got out of bed and into the shower. Choosing a pair of khaki Capri's and a sleeveless top that buttoned up the front, Allison dressed, and slipped on a pair of sandals. After putting on her make-up, she looked into the mirror and sighed. Then she pulled the door open and found Stephen pacing back and forth in front of her bungalow.

"What are you doing?" Allison pulled the door shut and walked toward him.

"Waiting on you," he said with a charming smile.

"You didn't need to wait."

"Yeah, I did. I wanted to apologize to you for last night," he said, as they started walking toward the restaurant.

"That's all right." Allison shrugged. "I'm sorry too, Stephen. I didn't mean to be so hysterical."

"I didn't think you were being hysterical, Allison." He put an arm around her shoulders and she looked at him. "Okay, so maybe I thought you were a little bit hysterical."

Allison laughed with him and punched him playfully in the stomach. "Friends then?"

"Yeah, we're friends. At least until I can convince you otherwise."

Marie McGaha

"I don't understand you Stephen," Allison said. "What do you want?"

"You wouldn't believe me if I told you," he said.

"Try me."

"You. That's what I want. I want you, Allison." She didn't say another word as they walked into the restaurant and joined their family.

"We're all just eating off the buffet," Captain said. "And we've got champagne flowing over here, too. Except for my blushing bride, she only gets juice for the next seven months."

Allison kissed her mother's cheek. "Hey, what about mine?" Captain pointed to a spot on his face, so Allison kissed him, and then sat down next to her mother.

"Get yourself a plate, baby," her mother said.

"In a minute," Allison said as she looked around.

"What's the matter baby?"

"I'd really rather order off the menu, that's all," Allison told her.

"Allison, what is wrong with you?"

"Look, Mama, I just want something off the menu, all right?"

"Sure. If that's what you want, but you don't get to eat—is that what this is about?"

"Yes, it is. I never go to the buffet because people stare at me. It's just easier to order off the menu."

Marie McGaha

"Allison, you are beautiful and you don't have anything to be ashamed of. So what if people stare, just tell them to mind their own business," Trudy said.

"Mama, I'm going to order off the menu, so please, let it drop," Allison said curtly.

"Fine. It's dropped."

"I doubt that," Allison mumbled under her breath.

"I heard that," her mother said, but she was smiling.

"I meant for you to."

"Allison, are you coming to the buffet?" Stephen asked.

"No, thanks. I'm going to order off the menu." She shot him a bright smile.

"They've got a great buffet," Captain said.

"I'm sure they do." Allison was ready to leave the restaurant altogether and get breakfast elsewhere by herself. Picking up a menu from the corner of the table, she waved to a server and ordered her breakfast, and coffee for herself and Stephen. The server brought two cups and an insulated carafe for refills.

Stephen sat down beside her and dug into the pile of food he had on his plate, and Allison tried not to pick off his plate while she waited on her order. When the waitress finally brought the Belgian waffle topped with strawberries and whipped cream, Stephen looked at her.

Marie McGaha

"Why did you order that off the menu? They've got waffles and stuff on the buffet."

"Thanks," she said sarcastically. "Can I eat now?"

"Sure." Unsure of how he'd made her mad again, he went back to eating in silence.

After breakfast, jeeps were rented for sight-seeing, and most of the day was spent tooling around the island doing mostly nothing, until Captain and Trudy had to take care of the marriage license. An opportunity Jason and Shelly seized upon to sneak back to their bungalow.

"What do you want to do?" Allison looked at Stephen. "We've still got hours before the wedding ceremony begins."

"I don't know. You want to go swimming?"

"Okay," Allison said non-committedly. She didn't really want be on the beach with all those bi-kini-clad tourists, but she couldn't see any way out of it. *Oh well*, she thought. If Stephen thought he wanted her, he may as well see what he was getting. "I'll meet you at my bungalow in twenty minutes."

Allison pulled the one-piece swimsuit out of the suitcase, held it up and sighed, wishing she were one of those bikini-clad women on the beach that Stephen wanted to look at. Having worn it on Cap-tain's boat, she had also managed to wear a pair of shorts all day to cover it, so Stephen had never real-ly seen her in the suit. Moreover, she really didn't want him to see her today, either. Pulling on the

Marie McGaha

suit, she also put on the white cover-up. Maybe she could wear it all day, she thought. Looking in the mirror, Allison thought she didn't look too bad with the cover-up doing its job. Stephen tapped on the sliding glass door, so she slipped into a pair of flip-flops and slid the door open.

"Do you have your sun block?" Stephen asked.

"Thanks, I almost forgot." She went back inside, grabbed the lotion and a towel, and went back out.

They walked to the water, spread their towels on the sand and sat down. Allison adjusted her sunglasses and watched people on surfboards as they attempted to ride the waves. There were women everywhere, and they weren't wearing bikinis, nope, these women wore rectal floss, with tiny swatches of cloth over their nipples, leaving nothing to the imagination.

Allison tried not to notice how most of the women noticed Stephen, so she lay down on her towel and closed her eyes. What did she care if he looked at women anyway? She opened one eye and looked at him. Even a woman six months in her grave would look at Stephen Collins. He was absolutely gorgeous, and now that all he wore was a pair of swim trunks, showing bronze skin stretched over taut muscle, was enough to make females of all species sit up and take notice. However, she reminded herself, he was with her, wasn't he?

"Hey, Al, I'm going in, you coming?"

Marie McGaha

"No, you go ahead," Allison said without getting up.

She waited all of two minutes before she sat up to watch him. Stephen was just being himself of course, but that alone was enough to draw women to him, and he smiled and laughed at the things they said. Allison watched, but she wasn't amused one bit.

When a buxom redhead kept putting her hand on Stephen's shoulder and throwing her head back, laughing, Allison picked up her towel and lotion and went back to her little room. Tossing the towel on the floor, she slid the glass door shut harder than necessary, peeled off the swimsuit, went into the bathroom and took a shower. Mumbling the entire time as she toweled off, she grabbed her robe and pulled it on. There were still three hours before the wedding, so she'd worry about getting dressed then.

And who had picked these tiny huts to stay in, anyway? Why didn't they even have a T.V.? Grabbing the paperback novel she'd brought to read on the plane, she lay down but couldn't concentrate on the book, so she tossed it to the foot of the bed.

Stephen opened the glass door and poked his head in. "Allison, why did you leave?"

She glared at him, but he came inside and shut the door behind him. "I didn't invite you in."

"What's the matter with you?"

"Nothing, now get out."

"No. Tell me what's wrong with you?"

Marie McGaha

Allison jumped off the bed and poked a finger in his chest. "You. You're what's wrong. You tell me you love me and then you can't wait to get out there with Ms. Redhead-In-A-Bottle. She had her hands all over you. You didn't need me out there for that. What did you do, tell them I was your fat sister?"

"You know what Allison? I've had enough of your insecurities. All you've done is be as difficult as possible, and treat me like I'm not good enough to wipe mud from your shoes. I have made it as clear as possible that I don't care how much you weigh, and I've told you that I love you, and I don't know what else you want. You told me we're just friends, and you told me to go find someone else to play with, and then you get mad when someone even talks to me. And for your information, I told the redhead you were my girlfriend. But you know what? I give up. You can take your insecurities and all that stuff about what Wesley did to you and... ah, it's a waste of my time!" He pulled the glass door open and stormed out without shutting it.

Allison stared at the empty space with her mouth open, then walked to the door and slid it shut. He was right, she thought. Everything he'd said was true, and she didn't know what to think now. And he'd not known, but when she told him she loved him, she meant it. She only lied when she said she thought of him as a friend. What did she want from him?

Just everything, that's all.

Marie McGaha

~ Fifteen ~

Allison lay on the bed and cried until a knock on the door interrupted her. She wiped her face and opened the door. Trudy came in carrying her wedding dress and a bag with all her accessories thrown over her shoulder.

"It's almost time, can you believe it?" she said, breezing past Allison. "I am so excited that I just can't believe it. Can you believe it?"

"Sure, Mama," Allison sniffed. "Captain is a lucky man."

"Captain? Oh no, baby, I'm the lucky one. That is the most wonderful, kind, generous, loving, caring man in the world. And he wants to marry *me*." Trudy began to cry.

"Why are you crying?" Allison hugged her mother.

"I don't know. Hormones from the baby or just the emotions from all of this." Trudy grabbed a tissue and wiped her face, then blew her nose. She looked at Allison whose nose and eyes were still red from crying. "What's the matter, baby?"

"Nothing. Let's get you ready now." Allison tried to redirect her mother's attention.

"Look at me, Allison. You've been crying. What's wrong?"

"Mama..."

Marie McGaha

Trudy sat down on the bed and crossed her legs. She had her mouth set and Allison knew that look meant no one was going anywhere until Trudy got what she wanted. Allison sat down beside her.

"All right. Stephen and I got into a fight. See it's nothing. Now can we get dressed?"

"What did you fight about?"

"Nothing, it was stupid."

"Allison Marie Hamstead, I don't have all day, now out with it."

"Stephen thinks he's in love with me and we've dated a few times, but I told him it wouldn't work out, and now he's mad at me. Are you happy?"

"Stephen's in love with you? And you don't have any feelings for him?"

"I'm in love with him, Mama, but it just isn't going to work."

"Why not? If you love him and he loves you, what can't be worked out?"

"Me. I just can't get past what Wesley and Sarah did to me." Allison stood and paced around the room. "I'm scared to trust him. And I keep thinking he's so handsome, so good looking, and he's dated so many women, what would he want with a girl like me, when he can have all the beautiful women that shake their rectal floss-clad rears at him?"

"Allison, I'm so disappointed in you. I know I raised you better than that. So what if he could have any woman he wants? If you're the woman he wants, what's the problem? And forget Wesley and Sarah.

Marie McGaha

Wesley didn't leave you because of your size, he's an idiot and he would have left you even if you were a size two. You can't let someone like Wesley keep you from happiness. What do you think would have happened if I had let all the years alone stand between Nelson and me?

"I want you to be happy, baby, with Stephen or without him, but make sure you base your decision on reality and not on something you've made up in your head."

"Thanks, Mama. Let's get ready for the wedding now, or Captain will be beating the door down trying to find you."

"He would, wouldn't he?" Trudy said with a dreamy little smile on her lips.

~ * ~

The ceremony took place as the sun set on the water, casting red, silver and gold across the sky as it fought its descent into the sea. When Captain kissed his bride, the family applauded, and so did others who had been on the beach and stopped to observe the scene. After the congratulations had died down, the bride and groom, with the wedding party in tow, made their way across the sand to a waiting limo for a tour of the island before taking everyone to the lovely hotel restaurant where a reception complete with cake, champagne, and a live band waited. The doors were left open. Soon people off the streets wandered in and a real party was underway.

Marie McGaha

Allison managed to avoid Stephen, but perhaps he was the one avoiding her, because he hadn't attempted to speak to her all evening. She sat at a table and watched her newly wedded mother dance with her groom and smiled at the sight. Jason and Shelly danced, and Allison watched as Jason said something in Shelly's ear. Shelly threw her head back and laughed, and then they kissed.

Allison felt her heart constrict. She wanted to be part of that sweetness, and she wanted someone to whisper in her ear and make her laugh so someone watching would wonder what he'd said to her. That was the kind of relationship she yearned for, and to know that secret language only lovers knew. She sighed and finished her glass of champagne. A hand holding a bottle of the bubbly wine came from behind her and filled her glass. Turning, she saw Stephen.

"Thank you," she said and attempted a smile.

"Mind if I sit?"

"No, of course not. Stephen, I want..."

"No, Allison, I want to say something first." He pulled out a chair and sat down. "I want to apologize for my outburst this afternoon. I shouldn't have yelled at you like that. There was no reason for it."

"I'm sorry too, Stephen. So, if you'll accept my apology, I'll accept yours. Deal?"

He held out his hand and she shook it. "Deal. Would you like to dance?"

Marie McGaha

Allison hesitated for just a moment before nodding. "Yes, I would."

He took her to the dance floor, holding her hand, pulling her to him as the band played a slow, sweet tune. Allison could feel the heat from his body as he moved her gracefully around the floor. His hand pressed against her back, his other hand held hers and he looked her in the eyes.

"I think you were the most beautiful woman on the beach this evening," he said.

Allison felt her cheeks heat. "Thank you."

"You don't take compliments well do you?"

"I haven't heard many of them I suppose," she admitted and averted her gaze. He made her feel very nervous.

"Take a walk on the beach with me, Allison," he whispered in her ear and she felt goose bumps rise on her skin. She nodded and he led her off the dance floor and through the crowd.

They walked down the wood plank walkway through the gardens to the beach. Allison slipped out of her shoes, and held them in one hand as Stephen held her other one. The moon was waning, but still cast soft light and lit their path. They wandered down the beach and gazed at the water as it lapped at their feet. Neither spoke for a long while.

"Do you remember the last time we walked like this?" Stephen looked at her as they walked.

"Of course I remember," she said. "You were drunk and threw yourself at me."

Marie McGaha

Stephen laughed. "That's not exactly how I remember it."

"Really? Your memory must be slipping," she said with a straight face.

"My memory, huh? So I just threw myself at you, did I?"

"Yes," she said. "You..."

He cut her off when he grabbed her and pulled her up against him. Looking into her eyes, he saw her surprise as he lowered his mouth to hers. The kiss wasn't soft, but neither was it demanding. He took a sip of her, tested the waters, and satisfied, pulled back. "Like that?"

She shook her head and pressed her lips to his. The fingers of her free hand went into his hair and her nails raked his scalp. Then suddenly, she pulled back and broke the kiss. "Like that."

"Hmm, I see," Stephen said thoughtfully. "Come with me." He pulled her along as he went and since they were closer to his bungalow, he stuck the key in the lock, opened the door quickly, drew her inside, then shut the door and locked it again.

Allison's heart pounded and she thought she might have a heart attack right then. Stephen cupped her face in his hands and kissed her. This time he demanded more from her, and she knew there was no turning back. She kissed him as if her life depended on it, because at that very moment, she wasn't so sure it didn't.

Marie McGaha

Suddenly, Stephen pulled back. He grinned and she cocked her head in wonder.

"This is what you've wanted all along, isn't it?" She asked him. "Here I am."

"Actually, it's not. Look, Al, I've been with a lot of women." He grinned when she frowned. "Now just hear me out. I've been with a lot of women, and some of them have been the model types, and some weren't, and yes, I did seek out women just like those on the beach today. But I never loved any of them. I never even came close to falling in love with any of them. You're the one I fell in love with. You," he said again, and pointed a finger at her heart.

"I fell in love with *who* you are, Allison, not how you look. But as far as that goes, I like the way you look. You have a wonderful body, and I don't want it to change. I love everything about you. And I decided to marry you a long time ago. I just didn't know how to get you to say yes. So I'm asking you now, Allison. Will you marry me?"

"I-I don't know what to say," she stuttered as tears leaked out of her eyes.

He rolled his eyes. "*Yes* is generally the appropriate response."

She nodded. "Yes."

"Thank goodness," he said. "I'd hate to think I bought this for nothing." He reached for the bed-side table, opened the drawer and withdrew a velvet box. Allison gasped when he opened the lid. The diamond reflected the light like a million suns.

Marie McGaha

"You bought that for me?"

"Of course it's for you." Grinning, he slipped the diamond engagement ring on her finger. "I love you, Allison," he said as he kissed her.

"I love you, too," she said against his mouth.

~ End ~

www.ingramcontent.com/pod-product-compliance
Lightning Source LLC
Chambersburg PA
CBHW070917130626
46555CB00001B/180